The Ghastling

"MENAGERIE"

TALES OF GHOSTS, THE MACABRE AND THE OH-SO STRANGE

EDITOR
Rebecca Parfitt
GRAPHIC DESIGNER
Andrew Robinson
EDITORIAL ASSISTANT
Tracey Rees
SOCIAL MEDIA MANAGER
Jen Smith-Furmage

SPECIAL THANKS
Heather Parr
J&C Parfitt

CONTACT
editor@theghastling.com
theghastling.com
Social Media: @TheGhastling

PUBLISHED BY THE GHASTLING

Copyright remains with the individual authors and artists. No part of this magazine may be reproduced, except for the purposes of review, without the prior permission of the publisher.

The Ghastling gratefully acknowledges the financial support of the Books Council of Wales.

ISSN: 2514-815X
ISBN: 978-1-8381891-9-8

THIS TWENTIETH ISSUE OF
THE GHASTLING
CONTAINS THE FOLLOWING WORKS

FAUN ... N.J. CARRÉ ... 11

A GRAVE FOR A DEAD HORSE ... J.P. RELPH ... 17

STACKING COFFINS ... JOSH HANSON ... 25

ONLY CARRION ... AVA DEVRIES ... 29

TEAR-SIPPERS ... VONNIE WINSLOW CRIST ... 33

MY GRANDMOTHER'S GLASS EYE ... ISOBEL LEACH ... 41

FREAKS ... FIONA CAMERON ... 49

BRAMBLE ... TOM PRESTON ... 57

LISTENING WOOD ... TIMOTHY FOX ... 67

ars longa, vita brevis

EDITORIAL

Thank you

If you're reading this: *Thank you.*

This is the section that I would usually call an Editorial — and it is — but as this issue is the twentieth issue and we are reaching the end of our tenth year, I just want to stop and take stock of how I got here, how I am still here, and what it means to move forward — carrying such a thing as *The Ghastling* with me.

I'm not joking when I say that I work alone in the small hours of the night. This is the only time that I can dedicate to the magazine — when everyone else is asleep. I suppose it's fitting, given the nature and content of the magazine. When I started this venture, it was on a whim. I wanted to submit my own work and I couldn't find a magazine that fitted the content. So I thought, why not start one? I already had plenty of experience working in publishing, it was easy, but I had no idea it would take off as it did. I started first as an online magazine but that wasn't enough, people wanted to hold it in their hands, collect it on their bookshelves. Covet it. After printing the first issue, I didn't look back. I found a rhythm and set a manageable print schedule of twice a year to allow for subscriptions and ten years later, here we are. Some of those first subscribers are still reading the magazine. However niche we are, we have readers and subscribers who have supported us from the beginning, that tells me I'm still creating something good.

This magazine means an awful lot of things to an awful lot of people. I have forged many relationships and many friends through its existence and what never fails to amaze me, is the support and sheer 'die-hard' commitment of our patrons, subscribers and readership. The kindness and generosity, the time people have volunteered to help me keep this going and to make this beast better has been overwhelming at times. I feel immensely proud to have created something that other people love so much. Build it and they will come. All the ghosts...

There have been times, particularly over the last six years that I thought I couldn't continue. The combination of the amount of work involved, caring for very young children, having a day-job and family commitments has proved too much for me sometimes. The continuing rise in costs for publishing, printing and postage is a constant worry. It often feels as though everything is stacked up against me and that alluring feeling of just dropping it, letting it go, not having these battles anymore has been very tempting.

But the reason I haven't is down to the people around me and my sense of pride of having built something that has given others a platform and also paved the way for more offshoots — other magazines and platforms for the genre. There is more opportunity with this beast, than without it, I suppose. We are a community of people who love the same things and that means something.

Will the magazine still be here in another ten years? I can't promise, but I hope so. The aesthetic and the aim will never change but we are evolving, with the generosity and skills of Alex Gillinder, we have started to experiment with audio which I would love to develop further (audio versions of some of our stories can be found on our Patreon page if you want to have a listen to what we have produced so far.)

And finally, I feel it is important to acknowledge the following people personally — people who have played an important part in the life of this magazine: my partner Gerald Alimon, for tolerating my mad whims and hair brained ideas. And for telling me that it is all possible. And making it so. To the good people of the Books Council of Wales for your continued belief and financial support over the years. The magazine couldn't continue without it. Mum and Dad. All of the extraordinary authors, artists, illustrators

EDITORIAL

and contributors who have featured in these pages, it is always such a pleasure to see people develop their craft and to showcase work. I never cease to be amazed by the quality of the stories submitted. To anybody who has ever taken a chance and bought a copy of the magazine, thank you. To the patrons past, present and future: I am eternally grateful for your generosity at a time when there is so much need in the World. Rhys Owain Williams, friend and ex-Ghastling ghost, for getting me through the difficult bits, especially. My current team of ghosts: Tracey Rees, Andrew Robinson, Jen Smith-Furmage and Alex Gillinder — thank you for your hard work and dedication to late night ghostly activity. The ghouls of Ghastlings past...

This issue is a paper menagerie: strange creatures from fauns and moths, to rabbits and vultures, fill the pages. It also features creepy children and teenagers doing dangerous things. Eerie landscapes, body parts with an independent agenda, disappearing and reappearing spectres, everything you need for an unsettling night... In 'Faun' by **N.J. Carré**, a woman living alone in a neighbourhood plagued by antisocial behaviour has a strange synergy with a creature she encounters in the woodlands by her house. Terrified, she begins to think the faun is sent to protect her somehow... 'A Grave for a Dead Horse' by **J.P. Relph**, the allure of a swinging rope hung above a deep pit is tempting for a group of early teens with nothing much else to do. But the game goes horribly wrong for one member of the party as her sister looks on — she could have stopped this, she should have stopped this, shouldn't she? And whose turn should it have been...? Another macabre children's game (they often are, aren't they?) leads these sadistic revellers to discover something far worse: Cheryl, the quiet friend, (because there's always one) is perhaps a little too quiet and a little too willing in this very creepy tale, 'Stacking Coffins' by **Josh Hanson**. **Ava DeVries**' story, 'Only Carrion', is a dark and brooding exploration of death and mortality. A woman receives visitations from birds after her miscarriage, and then, every time there is a death, a 'wake' of vultures begin to close in... In the brilliantly imaginative story, 'Tear-Sippers' by **Vonnie Winslow Crist**, professor Floella Greer, an ambitious academic and expert in *Lepidoptera* — in particular the variety of Tear-Sipping moths. Determined to forge ahead with her research plans despite the interventions of the misogynistic Professor Bogdan, she does something rather unethical to get her way... We've all coveted, cherished something belonging to a beloved relation. But what if it was really a part of them? In this eerie tale, a young woman inherits much more than a simple object: the glass eye seems to be in possession of its own sight in **Isobel Leach**'s 'My Grandmother's Glass Eye'. It is summertime in a seaside town, the light shimmers and Billy loves Laurel. They like to watch films together, sit together at school and avoid Spencer and the bullies. Everything is almost perfect, almost. But Laurel has a strange and occasional habit of disappearing — just not in the way you might think in **Fiona Cameron**'s story, 'Freaks'. On a miserable corner of the coastline, two old friends, Daniel and Bramble, meet to chat on a dilapidated bench overlooking the sea. But Bramble has the sensation he is being watched (pursued?) by a figure in a yellow raincoat, a figure sent to remind him of something he'd rather forget in **Tom Preston**'s tale, 'Bramble'. In **Timothy Fox**'s folk horror, 'Listening Wood', a young boy, raised by his father, haunted by the legend of his mother, keeps returning to the woods where she was found. A wood that only gives things up to those who know what they want. Tarnished by the name, Witch-boy, he struggles to line up to the ideals of what a boy should be.

And once more, dear reader, from the bottom of my black heart, I hold a goblet up to you in thanks.

Iechyd da!
Cheers!
Rebecca Parfitt *& the ghosts at Ghastling Towers.*

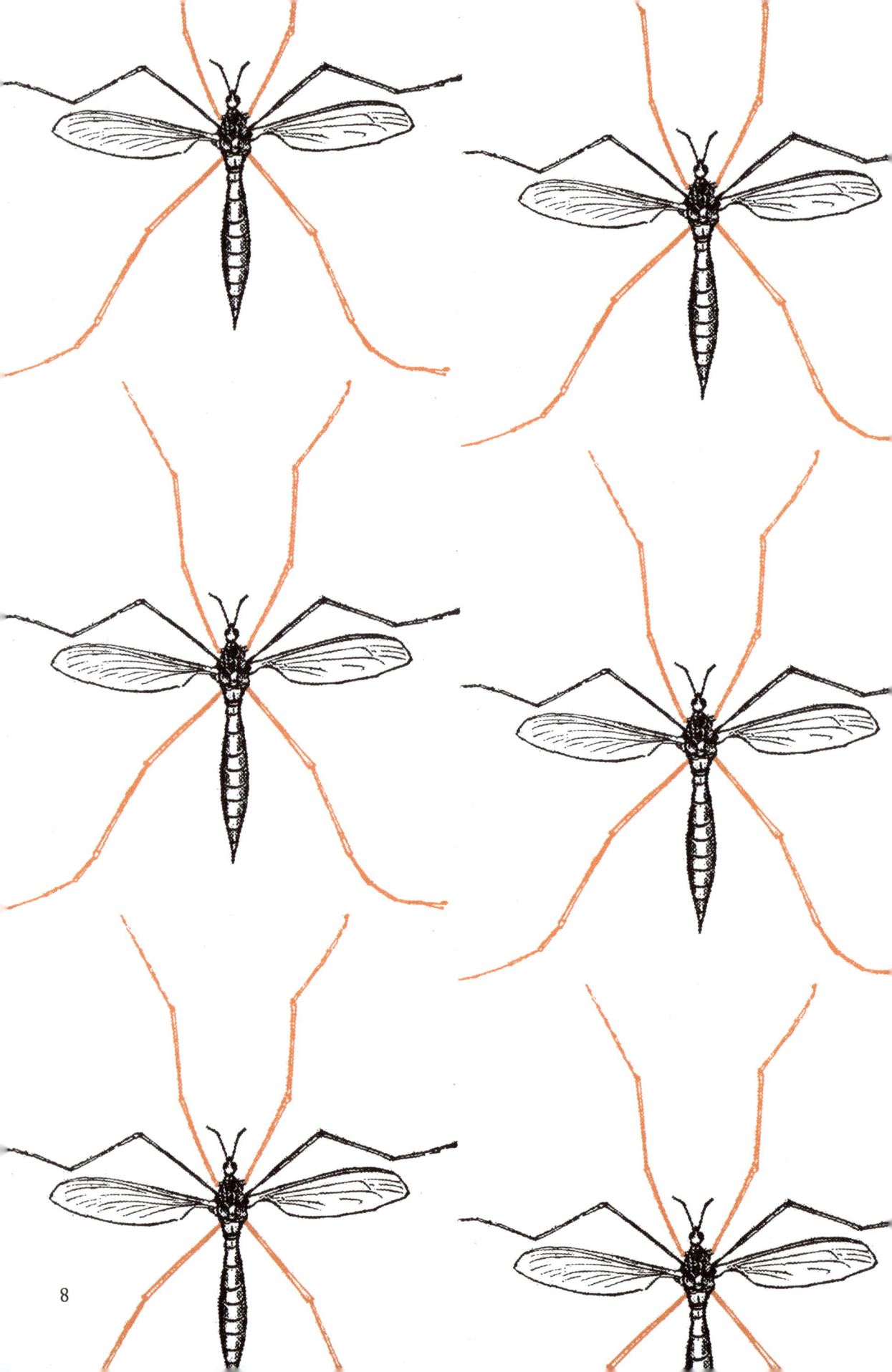

IF YOU YOURSELF WISH TO STAND ALONGSIDE THE PATRONS OF THIS CLUB VISIT
patreon.com/theghastling

ILLUSTRATION SKILLFULLY CRAFTED BY HEATHER PARR (*@xheatherlydiax*)

Faun

by N.J. Carré

It was the faun's eyes that pulled the breath from her, that stopped her dead on the track.

FAUN

There was an unease in the woods; the trees shifted then stilled as if they were unsure how she would react. Birds fell silent. She couldn't run, she was fixed to the last of the track. Panting slightly and with seized muscles she could only stare back at the pale yellow eyes watching her from the green, slotted pupils unmoving.

Of course she smelt it first, and curious, she followed what was barely a path, little more than trampled grass and weeds, briars pushed aside, leaning nettles. It smelled of freshly turned forest earth, ancient and root-riddled, specked with bones, oak galls and beech mast. She inhaled it all, intoxicated.

The faun stepped from the trees to the track. It was man from the waist up but goat below, shaggy black hair with sharp hooves tramping the briars. Her breath quickened but still she could not move. Except for the eyes its face was that of a man, lank hair to its shoulders. She studied it, all of it, wondered at the slight, indistinct protrusions on its head, the long nails, almost claws, curving at its fingertips.

It inhaled slowly, rhythmically, wisps of breath curling in the air between them. Her heart slowed too and she calmed, twitched her fingers and felt the blood warm. If there was fear, it had left her. She turned on the track, with high arms she picked her way through the nettles, then stopped to see what it would do. Its footsteps, softer than her own, followed. The track widened, the birds and the wood sounds returned and she paused twice more without looking back to hear the faun behind her. She understood she wasn't fleeing but leading.

The lads were at it again, out front in the car park and on the green. Across the road the shop closed early, the shutters pulled and padlocked. She watched it all from the gap in the curtains, lights off, everything double locked. Motorbikes first, engines squealing, rubber burning in tight circles then turf spewing from the back wheels, spattering the cars and houses. A white council van turned the corner at the end of the road, stopped then turned back again.

Then the fires. The lads, hooded grey and black, tipped over bins, pulled out rubbish and cardboard; set fires in the car park. They dragged pallets from skips, a stained mattress; piled them on the green, stuffed the gaps with newspaper. A hood leapt to the top, stamped hard on the pallets. He looks primal, she thought, back arched, arms flailing.

They tried to set the pyre alight; pale hands working at plastic lighters, their skinny fingers like bones flicking at the flints. They sparked but nothing took. A lad came with a bright red petrol can and dowsed the pile. It lit with a flash and the lads whooped and gaggled. They stomped around the fires, gobbing and pissing on the flames, maniacs dancing like wide-eyed marionettes.

She waited for it to run its course, for the bank of dark clouds to drift in over the rooftops. Rain came soon after, heavy drops arrowing down straight through the gloom. The pyre hissed, sputtered, tried to stay alive. The lads kicked at it, thin limbs unfolding and stretching, but it foundered, toppled dead in the downpour. Then they took off; one turned first then the others followed like a flock of black ash birds. They paled into the grey, sunk away into the alleys of the estate.

She pulled on her coat, went out into the back yard, to the broken fence that opened onto the rail line. She squinted through the rain, past the arc of the line, over the trees to the motorway, over the grey fields and linking hedgerows, shrouded now in swirls of rain. She searched beyond it all, looking for the hills in the murk, yearning for the woods.

The faun followed her a little further each time. She memorised the markers and the gaps — the slate grey ancient beech, the bank of curling willowherb, the swathe of nettles, high and strong, that sheltered the first and last of the track. She kept going back and it was always there, in the same place, hidden but for the eyes.

She wasn't sure what she wanted, why she was compelled to return, but she needed to breathe it, to be in the woods with it. Maybe that was all, maybe that was enough. But it came too and she wondered what it was looking for, if it was looking at all. Their meetings were elemental; there were no words or gestures, the only sounds from either of them were footsteps and soft breath as they walked.

It left her once at the holly tree that marked the gap in the hedge, came further next time into the field; stepped carefully through the furrows.

It came as far as the motorway then disappeared but a few days later it followed her through the stream beneath the flyover. She pushed her way through the old path behind the water treatment plant, only to emerge alone.

But it came further until, at last, it stopped at the track to the rail line. Here there were blasted stones, stained with fuel and oil; steel fences ribboned with barbed wire, litter trapped in the weeds. Still she wanted it to come further, just a little further. She wanted to lead it the best way she knew, out of sight like her, on the verge, along the tree line to the broken fence at the bottom of her yard.

But it always stopped where the track ended, dipped back into the woods without a sound. It didn't come, until one day it did.

When she left the shop there were three lads outside in the car park, slouched against a low car. She hesitated as she swung the shopping bag from one hand to the other, but the lads were up quickly. They buried their hands deep in their pockets as they walked over, spat in thin ribbons on the tarmac. The tall one flicked back his hood and smiled broadly at her. She looked down, sidestepped them, but they turned as a unit and followed her.

'You looking for some company?' Tall lad said, walking beside her. 'What's in the bag? Something for a nice romantic dinner?' One of the other lads sniggered. Tall lad leaned in close to her. 'Just the two of us. It'll be nice and cosy.'

She stepped away, slipped between two parked cars, and heard sniggering lad at her heels. The third lad blocked her on the path. She lifted her chin and looked at him; looked over his narrow face, his boy eyes. There's nothing there, she thought, he's blank, bloodless. There's nothing in any of them, just sallow skin stretched taut on thin bones.

She walked around the silent lad, quickened her pace towards a car swinging into the car park.

FAUN

At the corner she looked back. Two of them were back slouched on the low car, but silent lad was still on the path, empty eyes watching her.

The lads were out again and the faun was in the house. She led and it followed and now she didn't know what to do. It was curled, folded in the corner of the front room, head tilted to the drawn curtains, yellow eyes flicking from her to the window. She stood at the opposite wall, hands to her face.

It had come all the way at last; she kept going, didn't look back, knew without turning that it was there, close behind her. They came along the rail line at last light and it took three attempts before it ducked, soundless, through the broken fence and into the yard. Again, it hesitated at the door and once in the house it hunched, hooves skittering on the floor. She led it to the front room where it nestled itself in the corner.

What did she want from it now it was here? She wanted to breathe it in, but here wasn't the woods, here it smelt wet and rank. It seemed now more animal, more feral than before. It didn't belong, cowering there in the corner.

Outside, the lads piled pallets high and set the lot ablaze. They screeched like night foxes, guffawed and jeered, lobbed cans at cars. Low, deep beats shook the windows, throbbed through the floor. Fuel flashed on the fire and the room lit up orange, sending shadows into the house, amorphous shapes of lads wheeling on the ceiling. The faun flinched at the thud and scattering of broken bottles. She came halfway, dropped to her knees, eyes pleading with the faun not to leave but it rose, legs flailing like a new-born, it snorted earth and a low, guttural hum came from its throat.

She touched it. Her fingertips pressed lightly at its heart, just enough for it to stop and calm. They stood for a moment, linked, as blue lights flashed through the room and sirens screamed. A shadow fell between them and the faun stepped back into the corner. At the window, framed blue and orange, a hood shape grew. It could be sniggering lad, she knew, or silent lad or any of the others. More blue lights and sirens came, glass shattered to the dull beats, shouts and screams echoed, bounced off tarmac, chipped walls, scratched metal.

The front door shook suddenly; fists pounded the frame; the handle rattled to a blur; locks shook their casings; chains rattled. The hood shape was there now, shoulders rising and falling in the frosted glass.

'You in there, little piggy?' Sniggering lad pressed his face against the glass, distorted pale flesh, hard teeth. 'I'll huff... and I'll puff...' His sickening laugh poured into the shouts and wails. 'Come on, let us in, the cops are coming!' His fist slammed against the glass, cracks and fissures spread sharp and weblike.

The faun stepped to her. Its eyes changed, they looked into her and she knew it was telling her they had to leave. It paced to the back door, waited for her to open it, then they were out into the night. This time it didn't hesitate, it didn't falter through the gap in the fence and out onto the rail line. Behind them the sky flared orange and flashed hard blue, the shouts ebbed, became smaller and then they were at the start of the track.

The green was dark and thick and it pulled at them until their shapes were gone. It absorbed them. After a few moments her eyes adjusted to the gloom but she picked her way carefully, deliberately, keeping no more and no less than a half dozen paces behind the faun. She lost sight of it once or twice as it rounded the curves of the track but she knew it wouldn't leave her. The smell of the hedgerows filled her; elder drifted sweet on her tongue; hogweed bowed and bounced off her; stitchwort feathered her fingers; spider silk clung to her.

They left the track and the green and stopped beneath the flyover. She scratched nettle welts on the backs of her hands, wiped hedgerow dust from her eyes and lips while the faun squatted in the stream and cupped water to its mouth.

It suddenly rose, seconds before a figure pushed through the hedge from the field. A hood stood before them, frozen, fixed on the faun dripping in the stream. It raised its hand slowly and pulled back its hood and she saw the silent lad. There was enough light to see his eyes, wider than before and she thought there may be something there after all. She knew that if it was sniggering lad, or tall lad, or any of the other hoods they would flee, they would bring back others, hordes of them would come looking for them. But the silent lad could tell no-one. He's mute, he's silent, he sees like a ghost.

The faun stepped closer, straightened itself, made itself bigger. She also knew the faun could rake and maul, make short work of this silent lad. It tensed, they felt it more than they saw it. She reached and touched it again, fingertips to its shoulder and again it stilled.

She stooped and plucked a rock from the stream, briefly aware of the chill water flaring on the nettle stings. She stepped once, twice to the lad, raised her hand, held the rock high. The faun watched with yellow eyes, slots blinking slowly. Silent lad was a ghoul, mouth agape, wide eyes in terror until his blood rushed and he was gone, pushing into the green gloom of the track.

The faun stepped into the furrows and traced the line of the hedgerow. She dropped the rock and followed.

She understood it wasn't fleeing but leading.

A Grave for a Dead Horse

by J.P. Relph

It was that day I realised my nightmare was something else. Something portentous that saved my skin. I didn't know it would cost another. I didn't know for sure.

A GRAVE FOR A DEAD HORSE

We went to the pit that day. My sister and her friends had been before. It fascinated kids the way abandoned houses and graveyards do. Mum insisted Libby take me along; she was two years older than me, but it felt like loads more, like she was so grown up and I was still a baby.

The pit was just a big, soil sided hole in a field. Some locals say it was dug to bury a horse but never used. Others reckon it was going to be a trap for something, though they won't say what. The field belonged to a farm that nobody lived in anymore. Two old oak trees with knotty branches stood either side of the pit, like pub bouncers. The grass there was waist-high and sunburned. Someone once strung orange bail twine between the trees, as if it would stop kids going near. Rubbish had piled in the bottom, blown across from the nearby road, chucked in by older kids who came to drink and smoke at night. There was also a scattering of lost shoes; scuffed trainers and sandals, a couple of welly boots; fallen off when kids used the rope.

Branches from both of the oaks were entangled above the pit, providing a perfect place for some lad, three summers back, to crawl along and attach a rope. Enticing kids to swing over the pit. Dare each other. Timing it just right to let go of the rope and land on the other side, grabbing the tree so you didn't fall backwards.

I didn't want to go, not that day or any. It scared me — the thought of it being a grave still waiting for a body. All the shoes — making me think of snatched kids like on TV adverts.

There was also the nightmare: two nights before, me screaming so loud, mum came with a fire poker, thinking I was being abducted. I'd never dreamt anything so horrible. So red and real. I told mum it was just a bad dream about spiders. She laughed, made me warm milk.

Libby didn't want me to go either. She didn't want me around at all. She was wearing a bra that summer. Curling her hair and using pink lipstick. I knew she liked Tim; I'd read her diary. Picking the tiny brass lock with a kirby grip. Libby was thinking about kissing a boy and I wanted to stay home with my Barbies.

The others shrugged when we met them at the edge of the field, me shuffling behind my sun-gold sister like a stray puppy trying its luck.

'She's alright,' Tim said, making me blush for some reason.

Libby narrowed her dark blue eyes at me, said, 'You better not embarrass me, Tabby.'

It was hot, the sun hammering down on us as we crossed the field. I could see the corner where the pit was long before we arrived; it was deep in shadow. The trees there had few leaves. There was a smell wafting up that was dank and mushroomy.

I was sweating as we stood around the edge, staring down at the littered bottom. There was a chill to it, a feeling like winter wind puffing out. Roots that had breached the sides, found themselves with nowhere to go, hung like pale, dead snakes. I gripped the trunk of the oak beside me.

'Me first,' Tim said, untying the weather-faded rope that had been attached to the right hand tree by the last kid to use it. 'Then Graham.'

'Why always boys first?' A scrawny girl called Sharon asked.

Libby rolled her eyes, folding her arms across her bra-boosted breasts. 'Duh, Shaz. We need the boys to catch us if we get stuck.'

'Tabby can go after Graham,' Tim said, smiling at me.

I was miserable. Too hot, my hair stuck to my neck. My legs itchy from the long grass. I looked down into the pit, imagined bones there, just beneath all the crisp packets and pop cans. I saw my shoes — sunflower-yellow slip-on trainers — sticking up from the red-brown soil. My skeleton feet still wedged inside.

'Fine,' Libby said, coming up behind me. Her blond curls were frizzing, her cheeks as pink as her lips. 'Then me, then Sharon.'

Tim pulled the rope back as far as it would go, ran towards the pit.

'Go on Timbo!' Graham yelled.

I watched Tim's feet leave the ground. The rope strained, the branches above creaked and buckled. Then Tim was wrapped around the rope, suspended over the dark hole. For a moment I pictured teeth erupting from the pit's sides, snapping upwards. Pulling grey hi-tops from Tim's feet, severing his ankles. I shivered, pressed against the oak's hard skin.

'Don't be a baby,' Libby whispered harshly, before whooping at Tim as he let go of the rope. He was just over the far edge of the pit, his feet brushing grass. In the last seconds, he turned his body so when he landed, arms out, barely wavering, he was facing us.

'That's a TEN!' Graham shouted, grabbing the rope as it swung back towards us.

'Too easy!' Tim said, taking a bow. Everyone laughed. I tried, but it sounded off.

Graham went next. A clumsier, less acrobatic effort. Bark flakes fell from the branches above his head. He stumbled when he landed; crashed into the tree.

'Bollocks,' he said, rubbing at scuffed skin on his forehead.

Then everyone was looking at me. Tim with the smile so perfectly described in my sister's diary. Graham scowling, smearing spit over his graze. Sharon shaking her head, picking at a scab on her arm with dirty nails. Libby pouting, holding the rope out to me. Its long, frayed ends looked like a horse's tail. I chewed my lip so hard, it started to bleed. The metal taste spread over my tongue. Red as the nightmare.

'Seriously, Tabby. Don't make me look shit.' Libby's eyes were as cold as the pit.

'Come on, you'll be fine,' Tim shouted. 'We'll catch you.'

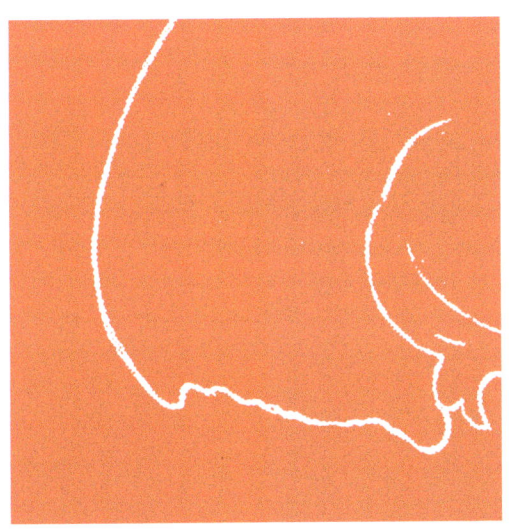

A GRAVE FOR A DEAD HORSE

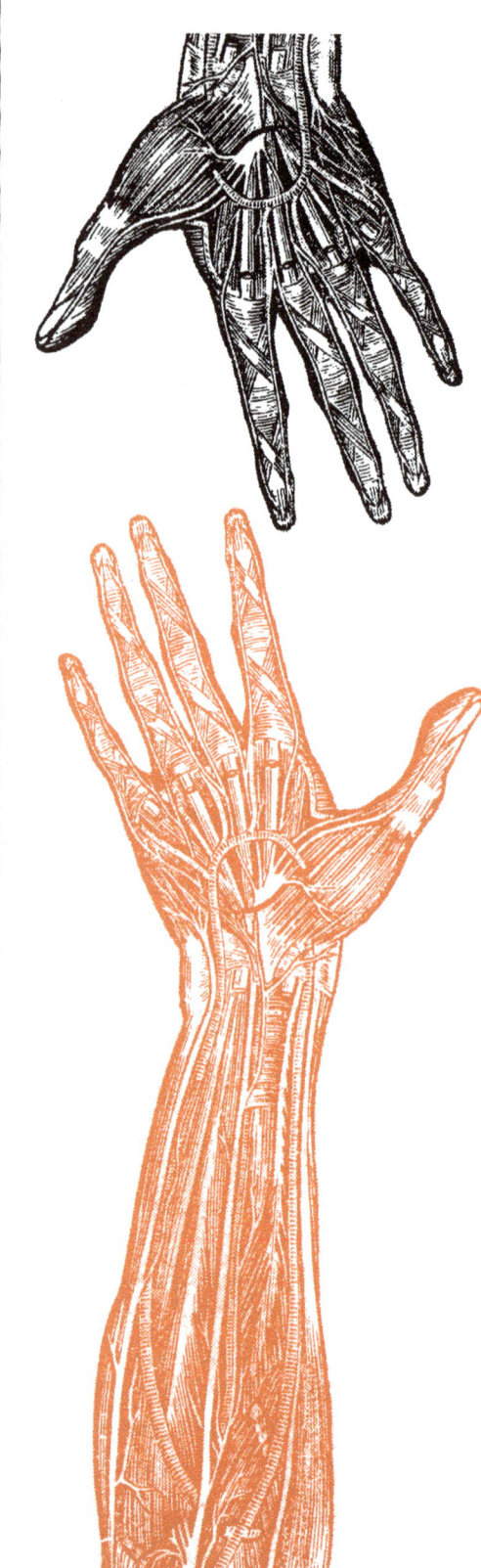

I thought of Tim's hands, hard-skinned and strong, around my calves, my thighs. My face burned in the tree-shade. My heart seemed to be in my throat. I took hold of the rope; it was scratchy, unyielding.

'I'll push you if you want?' Sharon said, grabbing the waistband of my shorts.

I looked at my sister, the disgust on her sun-puffy face. Something else there too: fear. Making lines at the corners of her mouth. She was scared that I'd make Tim not like her. By being a baby. An embarrassing sister dragged into her fantasy of them as boyfriend and girlfriend.

I looked down into the pit, closed my eyes; I could feel the cold soil on my skin, crumbling around me, threatening to bury me. My arms and legs splayed and snapped. The back of my head squelching. I smelled the blood, the piss on my shorts. Heard all the screaming.

I let go of the rope, shoved my hands into my armpits to warm them. I shook my head so hard, sweat flew into Libby's face.

'I don't believe you, Tabby,' she snarled, 'Why did you come?'

'You made me,' I said, which was cruel.

'It's fine,' Tim shouted. 'Maybe next time. Come on Libbs, you take her turn.'

'I hate you sometimes,' Libby said, snaking her hands up the rope. Then she turned to the boys, grinned with all her teeth, and launched.

The rope seemed to shudder as she left the ground. Libby spun wildly over the pit. She was laughing though, showing off, wrapping her thin legs around the jerking rope, her skirt riding up. I heard the branches crack, showering her in chips of wood.

'Shit, guys,' she cried, her laughter stuttering. She'd lost momentum.

'Help her,' Tim yelled, reaching out.

Twigs snapped free of the branches, got tangled in Libby's hair. I could see the strain in her face, the tendons in her arms. She was twirling dead centre above the pit.

'I can't reach her,' Graham shouted. He was leaning out as far as he dared, as was Tim. Suzanne had run round to their side of the pit, was just standing with cupped hands over her mouth. I dropped to my knees, crawled to where grass ended and a black nothingness began. My hands clawed into the soil. Bloody saliva dripped from my mouth.

'Libby, come back,' I said too quietly for anyone to hear. 'I'm sorry.'

'Grab my shirt, Graham, I'll get further out,' Tim said. Panic making his voice high, his eyes washy. He got closer to Libby, tried to snag her top, her skirt. His trainers poked over the pit's edge. Graham's face was scarlet as he held Tim's t-shirt in a white fist, his other arm hooked around an oak branch.

Libby was crying, snot bubbling from her nose. Her hands kept slipping down the rope; it burned her knees where they squeezed it. She cried out. Dropped down until she was waist-deep in the shadows of the pit. Tim managed to get a few fingers wrapped around the strap of her vest top — it stretched as he pulled.

'Got her!' Tim shouted in hysterical glee.

The branches overhead seemed to untangle from each other. A horrible crack, loud as a TV gunshot, and the rope simply fell. Libby hovered for impossible moments as it ravelled past her, her blue eyes wide and wet.

'Tabbs,' she said, her voice like breaking wood, and then she fell too.

'Go get help!' Tim yelled at Graham, who nodded, sprinted away across the field.

The nearest place was a pub, The Bay Horse. It would be open for lunch, had a phone.

'Libby! Are you hurt?' Sharon shouted, her shoulders shaking with sobs.

My sister only groaned in response. She was sprawled on her back amidst all the nasty rubbish and shoes. I could see red-striped bone poking from her left ankle. Her right arm was bent up behind her, the shoulder bulging. Something that caught the sun like water was jutting from her neck, everything around it glossy red.

> *'Tabitha,' she murmured and my heart broke. Nobody had called me that for years.*

Libby's eyes fluttered open and closed, open and closed, like dark blue sky glimpsed through blinds. 'Tabitha,' she murmured and my heart broke. Nobody had called me that for years.

'It's ok, Olivia.' I lied, swiping tears from my face with soil-smeared hands. 'Someone's coming.'

I thought of mum that morning telling Libby not to be mean, to spend more time with me. *You'll both be grown up soon and wish you'd been closer*, mum said. Libby had snorted, cereal scattering off her spoon, *yeah, yeah, mum, whatever*. She's already grown up, I wanted to say. She has a bra and lipstick and writes about snogging a boy. I'm never growing up. It's too hard.

The field was gravely silent. There was no birdsong, no clicking of bugs in the hedges. Tim was rocking back and forth, his head on his knees. A scrap of Libby's peach cotton top was clenched in his hand. Suzanne was still crying, leaning her head against the oak. I was the only one looking down.

Libby's chest was soaked red, many of her frazzled curls turned pink. Her broken body was still, her mouth slightly open, her eyes closed. The pit seemed to sigh in sorrow, wafting winter air against my face. It dried my tears. In the vision two nights before — and I knew then it was a vision and not just a nightmare — it was me in the pit. Red, red pain and so much blood. One shoe off and one at a terrible angle. It was me dying in a horse's grave.

Mum didn't let me out of her sight for the rest of summer. I was content to be in the house; living my life through my Barbies and their adventures. The funeral had been all pink coffin and *Olivia* spelled out in pink roses, Libby's friends in stiff black trousers and skirts, cold quiche. Mum asked me that morning if I wanted to put something in the coffin with Libby; a favourite old toy or a letter. I placed her diary in the crook of a cold elbow. I felt she should take her words, her fantasies and hopes with her.

The council built a metal cage around the pit, planned to fill it eventually. Some kids still hung out there, climbed the cage like monkeys, dropping flaming rags into the pit's cold depths. Kids are stupid. Even when someone dies. It doesn't touch them, teach them. They want to poke at snakes, run over fires, swing over pits with broken glass hidden in the bottom. They want to live fast, even if it means brushing up against dying.

Another summer, another town, another bunch of stupid kids. My friends this time. I'm the age Libby was when she died. All grown up. I wear a first bra under my t-shirt, a tinted lip-gloss that tastes of strawberry. Mum says I can go out if I'm careful; she's gotten tired of coddling me. She fills the house with vases of pink roses, tells me to take juice.

I meet the others on the bridge over the river. The water sluggish today, barely frothing as it moves over flat stones. We throw sticks in it for a while, see whose makes it to the other side first. The sun hammers down on our backs, frizzing the curled ends of my hair.

When Brett suggests we go to the tracks, I close my eyes, dig my nails into the bridge's wooden railing. Cathy and Simon are up for it of course; they link arms and start walking.

'Tabbs?' Brett has eyes like the ocean on postcards, brown-sugar skin, a crooked smile. I write about him in my diary.

I smile, say, 'Coming.' Light as sunshine on water.

I've had other visions in the last two years. Visions of me in terrible situations; badly injured, dying. Only ever me. A selfish precognition you could say. I knew to avoid crossing the street by my school at four-o-clock on a Friday in September. There were roadworks, cones in place. A bread truck driver on his phone, distracted, angry with someone. He plunged through the cones, smashed into the school fence. Two kids were injured, one's in a wheelchair now.

I also knew not to skate on the frozen lake in December or swim in it in April. Not to ride my friend's skittish horse in February when black ice hid on the road or in June when a speeding car sideswiped it. Twice this year, I've known to stay clear of the derelict barn outside of town where kids like to let off fireworks.

Death keeps coming for me. Seeming ever more eager. Something else keeps warning me and, in heeding those warnings, someone else always gets hurt. Like Libby.

We're down by the tracks, heat pluming from the metal, the gravel under our trainers is sun-baked. I push my hair off my face, tie it in a scruffy bun. Brett is doing lunges, making us laugh. We all know Simon is the fastest. When I close my eyes, I can hear the scream of the train braking, the screams of the others. I can feel gravel gouging my cheek, see my purple trainer, spattered with thick blood, next to my head. My foot still inside it; skin like a frilled sock, trimmed red.

When I open my eyes, Brett's there on my left. Grinning and golden. Ducked down in a starter position. Cathy and Simon are further along, spread a little apart, staring up the long stretch of sun-silvered track. The shimmying air parts like dense curtains, a muggy breeze blasting over us all. It's coming.

'Get ready,' Brett shouts, his feet scuffing the gravel like a horse about to race.

The train rounds a bend in the distance. The rails in front of us buzz, the ground shakes.

'READY!' Brett shouts again, raising his arm, hand clenched in a fist. His voice snatched by the bellow of the yellow-faced beast bearing down on us.

We never see the driver — the sun always on the windscreen — but we always joke about the look on his face. About whether he shits his pants. The train's roar is immense, we watch Brett's arm for the signal — when it drops, we'll go. Cathy and Simon focus on it, straining not to look at the train. They'll never go before Brett. Being at the front of our line, I have to look away from the thundering train to see Brett at all. He says that makes me even more badass.

Hair escapes my bun, sticks to my sweaty cheeks. I taste the grit being spun in the air. No sweetness of strawberry left on my lips. I think of a pink coffin and my name spelled in roses. I think of mum saying *You'll both be grown up soon and wish you'd been close*. I shouldn't have grown up.

I don't look at Brett's arm, I stare at his eyes. Intense, ocean-blue that I can never capture when I sketch in my diary. None of my pens are right. He glances at me once, his smile beautiful, before looking past me again. When his arm drops and the train is on us and three lithe bodies dart in front of it, I take one step back, then another. I don't hear the sound of metal on meat, or the screaming of brakes and blood-spattered kids for long, long moments. All I hear is my own blood crashing in my head. I drop down into grass, wrap my arms around my knees, stare at my clean purple trainers. The train driver is running up the tracks, his face stark grey-white, his mouth wide open. I don't look at the mangled mess. I know how red it'll be. The coffin though, this time it'll be blue.

Death keeps coming for me. Seeming ever more eager. Something else keeps warning me. If I choose it, someone else always gets hurt. I didn't know a year ago when I stepped aside and let my sister take my turn on the rope. I didn't know for sure that a nightmare was really a vision of the future. My future. My death. I've known for sure a while now. That out there is my grave, dug and waiting. I guess I want to keep growing up.

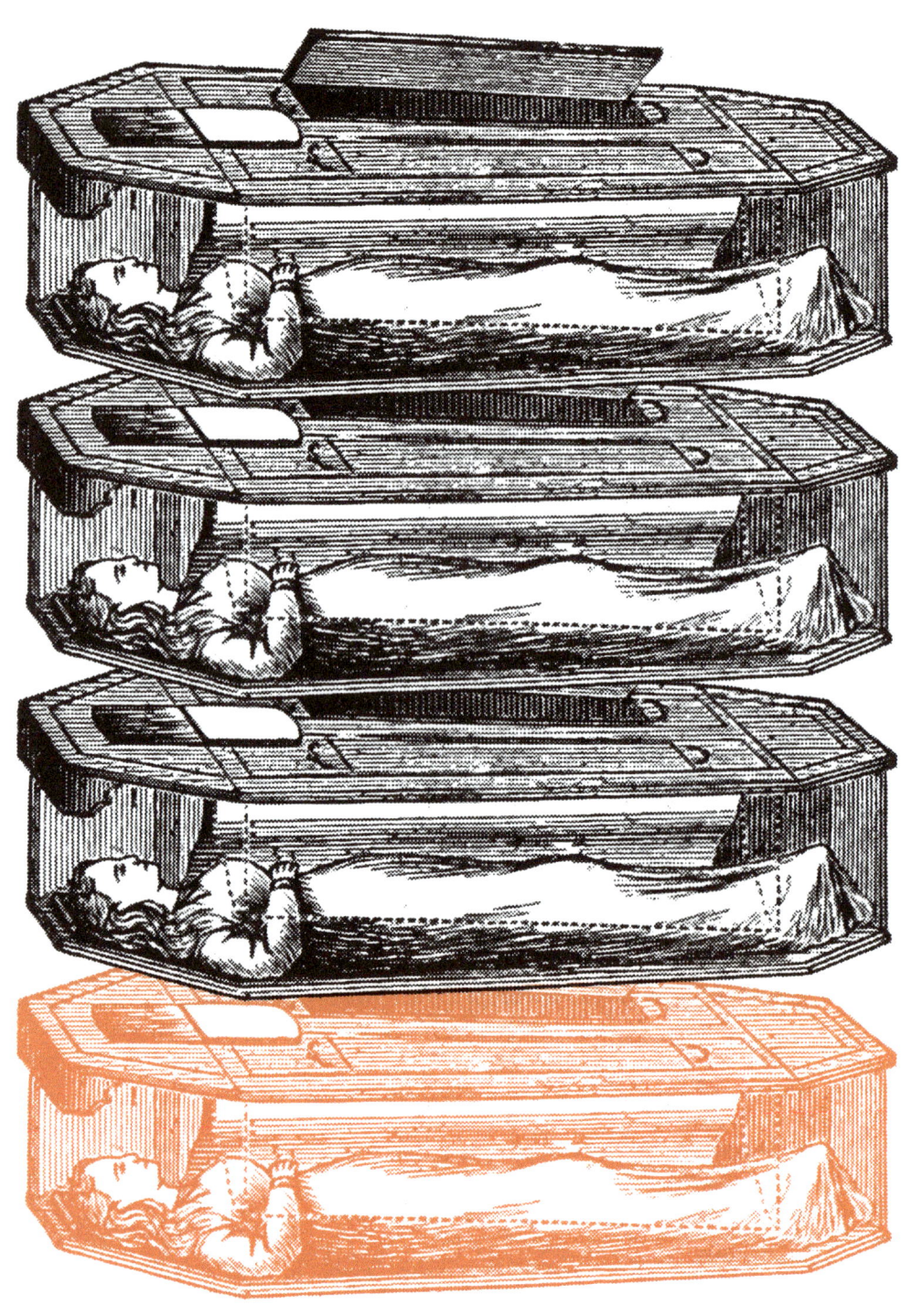

fig. 2-126

Stacking Coffins
by Josh Hanson

The game was simple.
James and Eric dragged out their big matching toy boxes, heavy plywood things wrapped in cotton batting and then covered with naugahyde.

James' was blue. Eric's was gray. We'd put one of the boxes in the middle of the room, and someone would climb inside. The lid was shut, and then the other box was stacked on top. Someone would climb inside that box. Then we would stack as many things as we could find on top: an ottoman, couch cushions, blankets. Bury the whole thing like they were Egyptian royalty. Usually, someone would climb up on top. Usually that someone was James, him being too big to fit inside the toy coffins and him being naturally sadistic. We liked to play with James because he was older, but he frightened us in equal measure.

And that was stacking coffins. You stayed inside until the panic finally began to flutter in your chest, and then you screamed and pounded on the inside of the box way down there, under the weight of the whole world, and eventually the mountain would be cleared away and you'd be resurrected, laughing and gasping.

But not Cheryl. Cheryl wouldn't make a sound. We'd eventually scatter the pillows and blankets, remove the stray furniture, lift down the top box, and open the lid to find her lying there, curled on her side, as if sleeping. She liked the dark, she said, and the quiet. The closeness calmed her, made her feel safe.

So Cheryl wasn't much fun, but we made her play anyway, because everyone had to play. Those were the rules. Everyone but James, who ran the game.

The day it happened, Cheryl had been crying. We saw that right away. Red eyed and sniffling, she sat in front of the television, watching a rerun of *Solid Gold* with three dancers dressed in contrasting black and white outfits. We sat down and watched quietly, knowing not to ask, not to push. Cheryl would come around. She always did.

James came into the room, seeming shocked to find us there, but recovering quickly. He leaned on the back of the big recliner where Cheryl sat with her legs tucked up under her, and he rocked the chair back and forth, slowly at first, then faster.

Finally, when the chair's movement became too violent, Cheryl clutched the arms and gave a little squeak of pleasure. James laughed, and we laughed, happy in the knowledge that James had broken the spell; returned Cheryl to us from that dark, distant place she sometimes disappeared to.

James stilled the chair, Cheryl still clutching the arms, ready for the real possibility that he would suddenly send it into motion again. But James was done. He leaned on the chair's back, half-watching the dancers on the TV, and then, without looking at anyone, he said, "Let's play coffins."

Eric and I ran to drag out the boxes, and soon we were in the darkened living room, the summer sun seeping yellow-brown through the thick curtains. I'd never seen those curtains open. This room was always darkened, the furniture mostly unused. I went first into the bottom coffin, hungry for that little death, that moment of stillness that would shift suddenly into panic. I wanted the panic. That was the draw of the game — the quiet and the panic, they were both a kind of surrender.

And then it was Cheryl's turn to go in.

In my memory, I like to believe that she gave some meaningful look, that she squeezed my hand before the lid was lowered, but that's all fantasy. She just curled up on her side, looking

I knew Eric was okay inside. Nothing could hurt him. There was plenty of air.

straight ahead, and then we were gleefully stacking things atop the box. This time, as he sometimes did, James arranged the items into a kind of throne, two blankets thrown over it, and he sat atop the tower, his head nearly to the ceiling, and peered down at me, arms resting on his knees, in his best approximation of Conan.

Eric was in the top box, and it didn't take long for him to begin to pound and kick. But James acted as if he couldn't hear. He turned his head from side to side as if he were taking in the limits of his kingdom, heedless to the cries and muffled pounding from below.

Eventually it was clear that Eric was genuinely frightened. We could hear the wet sound of his crying, the asthmatic wheeze of his cries, so James slowly climbed down off of his throne and pulled the blankets down after him. I rushed forward to pull down the pillows. I knew Eric was okay inside. Nothing could hurt him. There was plenty of air. But I also knew the sensation of that box contracting around you, the delicious, terrible fear of it, so I worked quickly to uncover him, to let him out.

He came out angry, with snot smeared across his face, ready to fight, but of course James was twice his size and, utterly remorseless, would twist Eric's arm to the breaking. So, finally, he just sulked and kicked at the discarded bedding.

James and I finally removed the top box.

As always, Cheryl was silent inside, waiting, happy in her cocoon of dark. I pictured her sleeping, oblivious to the noise and emotion outside of her little coffin, cornsilk hair fallen over her round face, lips parted slightly.

He opened the lid, to find the box empty, Cheryl gone.

Eric came forward, looked between the empty box and James, his face a blank, and then finally spoke.

"James," he whispered. "What did you do?"

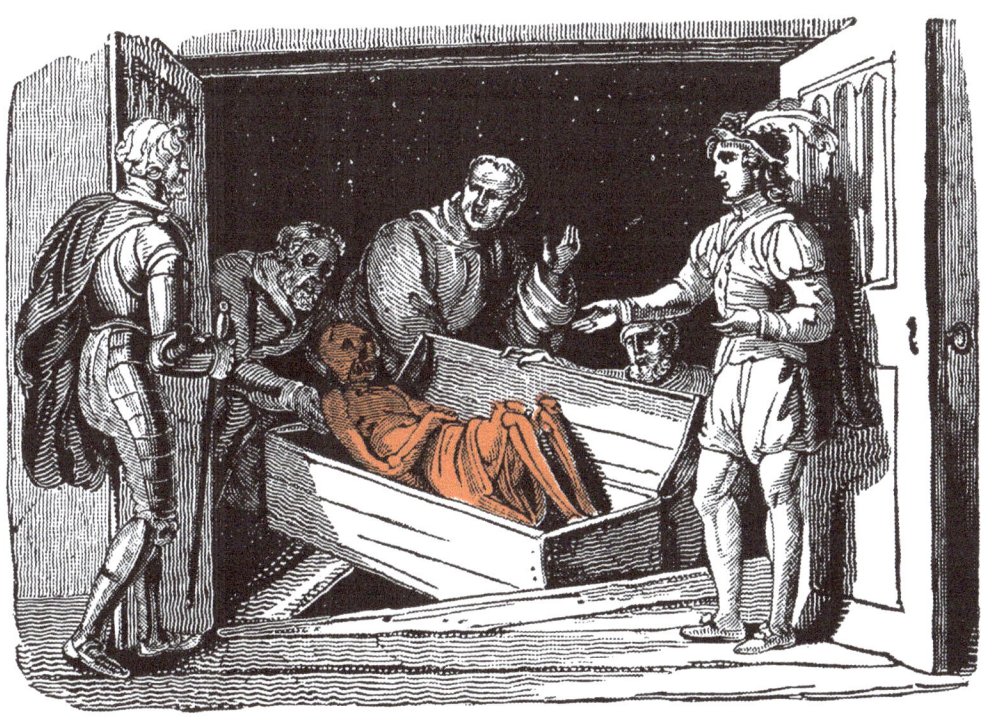

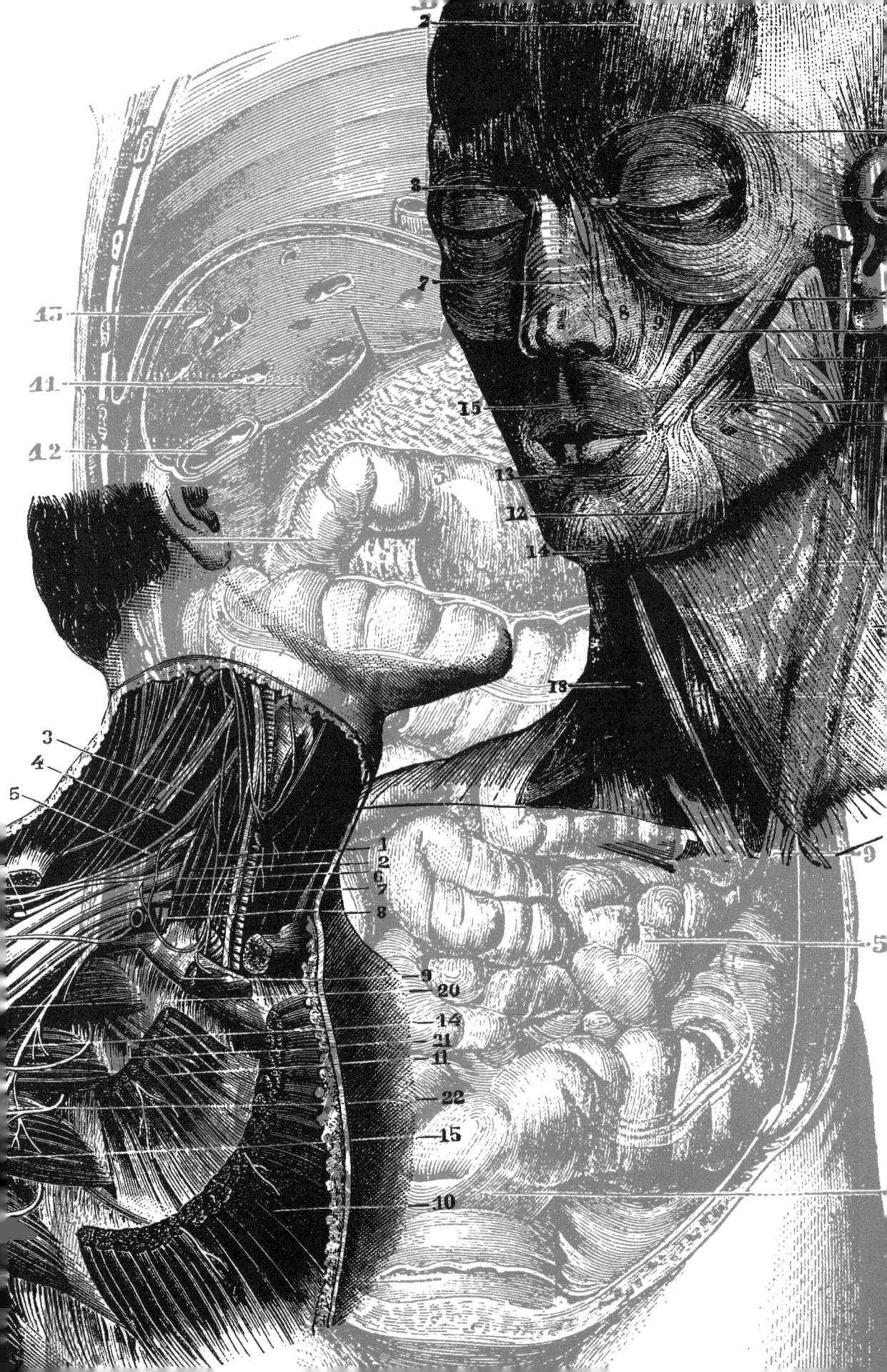

Only Carrion
by Ava DeVries

The vultures have been gathering around my house again. Only three or four, for now. But more will be here soon. They will perch on my picket fence and roost on my roof until it creaks with the weight of them.

ONLY CARRION

The first time I saw them was just after my miscarriage. I came home from the hospital to still-stained sheets and a fat black bird waiting atop my mailbox, its red face puckered and expressionless. More began to show up in the days, then weeks, then months that followed, finally culminating in my husband's exasperated departure. When they did eventually dissipate, melting away to haunt some other house, it was months before I stopped finding feathers caught in my hair or stuck in the wool of my cardigans. My house felt lonely, then, without their blanketing presence.

But that was years ago. I'm not sure why the vultures are here now. I ask one of them, waiting just outside my kitchen window. *Why are you here?* It doesn't answer — only peers at me through one beady, sludge-black eye.

When I was much younger, no more than seven or eight, I picked up a *National Geographic* magazine about scavenger species. I remember reading that a group of feeding vultures is called 'a wake'. I thought nothing of it until years later, when my grandmother died unexpectedly, and I overheard my mother on the phone discussing funeral arrangements. *We'll have to find a nice pair of shoes to put her in*, she was saying, *for the wake*. I remember bursting into panicked tears upon hearing the word, suddenly imagining a procession of mourners descending upon my grandmother's open casket, feasting on her wrinkled body. Imagining myself among them, forced to bite, chew, *consume*.

After the funeral service, my mother and I drove home in silence. I couldn't stop picturing my grandmother's placid face as it had looked during the wake. A dark shape flickered at the edge of my field of vision, and my mother whispered *don't look*, but I had already seen the deer lying dead on the side of the road. It must have been struck by another car. Such a sorry, bleeding thing. There was a single vulture feeding on the carcass, the animal's ribcage white and exposed in the late-afternoon light. I thought I should have been disgusted; I thought I should have looked away. Instead I felt a morbid sort of fascination. Here, there were no silk-lined caskets. There were no embalming fluids pumped through still veins. Here, the dead fed the hungry, and the hungry felt no remorse. Here, the dead served a purpose.

I dream of blood between my thighs, crimson-wet. I dream of my skin prickling with what I think is gooseflesh, before it erupts into dark feathers. Of ripping into dead flesh, putrid and delicious. I dream of my husband. He used to look at me with such love. Such aching desire. Now he only looks at me with—what? Disgust? Pity? I dream of eating his insides.

ONLY CARRION

In the morning, I can hear the creaking voices of the vultures calling to me from all around. My reflection in the mirror shows no evidence of my nighttime metamorphosis. My skin is smooth and unmarred.

I make myself a cup of strong black coffee, as I do each morning. There is a vulture on my kitchen counter; I wonder how it got inside. We regard each other with muted interest. When I am finished with my coffee I wash the mug, dry it. Put it back in its designated spot in the cupboard above the sink. Strip my clothes off, let them fall to the tile floor. Walk into the back yard. Let the chill of the morning shock my naked skin. Lie down. Wait.

I stay there on the ground for so long, I swear I can feel myself begin to rot. I can see more of them gathering in the surrounding trees, one by one, dark smudges against the dust-colored sky.

They observe me from above like angels. Finally, as if following an inaudible summon, they begin to descend. Their beaks pierce my skin, open me up to the cold air. They tear at my liver and stomach, squabbling over the organs like children. They pick my ribs clean, feast on the meat of my breasts. The sinew of my legs and arms are torn away in strips. They pluck my eyes effortlessly from their sockets and get to work on my tongue. I am bones. I am flesh. They reach the pulsing muscle of my heart, and then I am nothing at all.

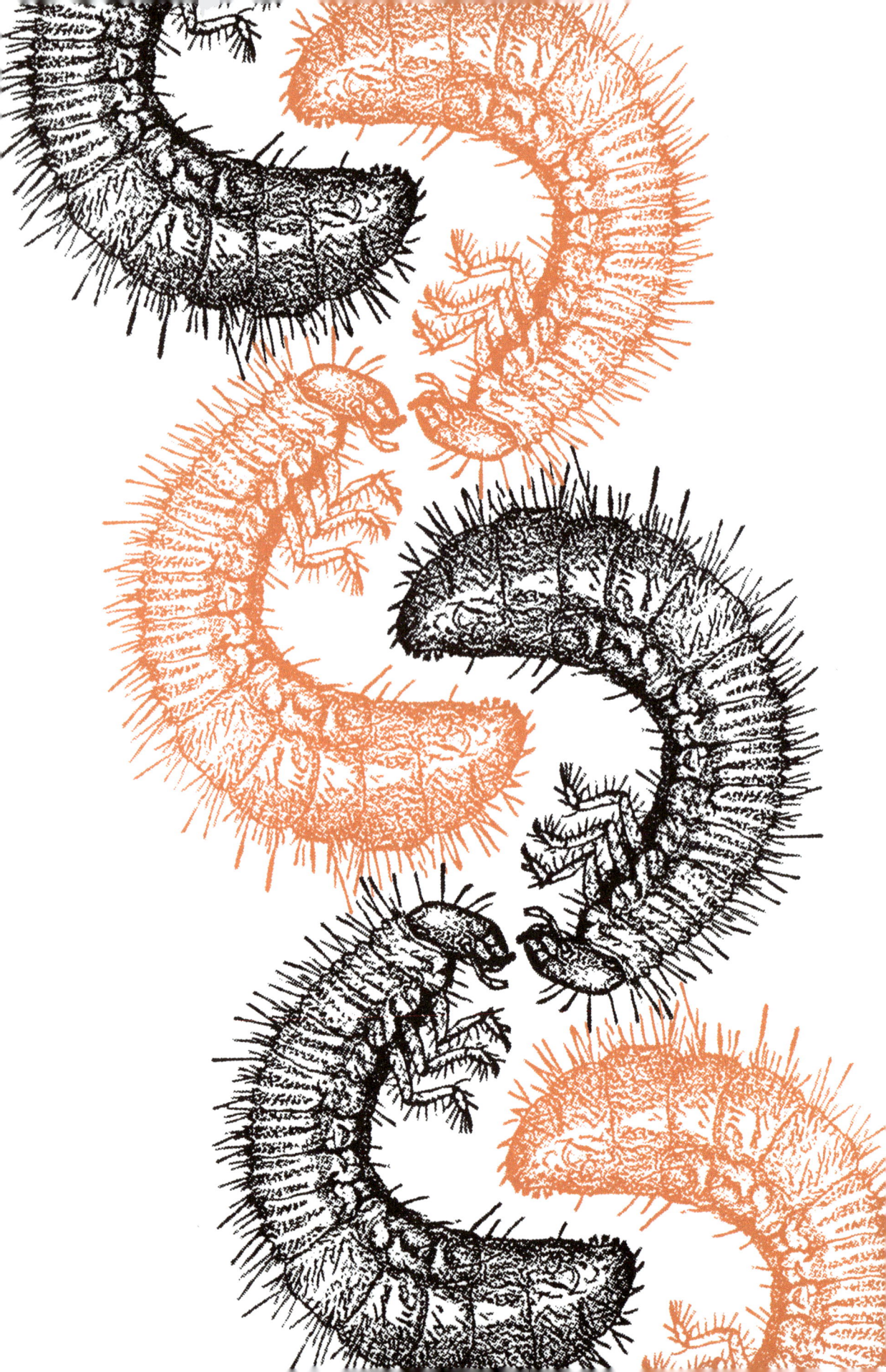

Tear-Sippers

by Vonnie Winslow Crist

Professor Floella Greer kissed the air directly above a moth balanced on her finger.

TEAR-SIPPERS

As if the kiss was what it was waiting for, the insect then fluttered to a shadowy corner of the room. With grace befitting such a lovely creature, it silently landed on the wall. Pale wings spread; the moth nearly blended into the wall. It comforted Floella to know, just like the seen and unseen angels in the architecture of cathedrals, the moth and its magic were still there.

Infatuated with moths since childhood, Floella identified with their role as the chubbier, night-loving cousins of diurnal, brightly hued butterflies. Monarchs, swallowtails, fritillary, and the rest of their daytime kin were celebrated in stories, songs, and legends. Moths, not so much. But Floella knew butterflies and moths were creatures cut from the same cloth, with little separating them but clubbed antennae.

A knock on her office door halted her musing.

"You in there, Flo?" asked a gravelly voice.

"Yes, Professor Bogdan," Floella responded pleasantly, though it required effort to do so. The man never acknowledged her in a professional manner. But today, it was counterproductive to annoy Wallace Bogdan by reminding him she was a professor, too. "Please, come in and sit down."

"I'm here for the tea, biscuits, and conversation you promised," stated the portly man in a three-piece, tweed suit as he strolled into her office. With a loud, "Humpf," he settled into a leather armchair opposite her desk. "I must say," added Professor Bogdan after an exaggerated survey of the room, "your office is quite eclectic."

Floella smiled. "I have collected moths since childhood and enjoy displaying my pinned collection."

She glanced around the room. Dozens of framed displays of carefully collected, preserved, and labeled moths from across the world decorated every inch of the walls not occupied by bookshelves crammed with books on *Lepidoptera*. The drapes on her office windows, rug on the floor, and upholstery fabric on the room's other three chairs also featured moths and butterflies. Even the light switch covers had moths painted on them.

"I guess my hobby, my area of interest and expertise, and my passion are on full display," she replied with a smile.

"I would say it is overdone. A bit garish for me." Professor Bogdan waved his fingers in a dismissive manner. "But for you, perhaps it is just right."

Floella pressed her lips together. Eyelids lowered slightly, she placed a napkin, silver teaspoon, and a small China teapot, saucer, and teacup on the table beside his chair. The China, decorated with delicate paintings of moths and butterflies, had been a birthday gift from her late mother. Mum had ordered the tea set from a Czech manufacturer of specialty China.

"Sugar? Cream?" inquired Floella as she straightened her back. She forced a smile.

"Yes, both," responded Bogdan with a sniff. He checked his watch, then sighed loudly.

He's a bloody idiot. I don't know why I thought he'd support me in securing research funding for my study of lachryphagy, she thought as she held a tray with a creamer, sugar bowl, and plate of shortbread cookies in front of her colleague.

Wallace Bogdan helped himself to two lumps of sugar, a generous dollop of cream, and four cookies.

"Ah, wait a moment." He licked his lips. "Perhaps, I will have another cookie." He selected two more pieces of shortbread from the China plate, laughed, then added, "Maybe I'll have two for good measure."

34   *THE GHASTLING*, BOOK TWENTY

Noticing that once again the septuagenarian failed to thank her for her hospitality, Floella placed the tray on her desk. She sat down in her desk chair and poured some India black tea from *her* pot into her teacup. She added no cream or sugar.

"As you know, I have been studying lachryphagy among *Lepidoptera* for several years now," she began. "I would like to continue my research both here and abroad. As a valued colleague, I was hoping I could count on your support with the University. If you..."

Bogdan raised his right hand. "Before I offer any sort of support, I think we need to discuss this whole tear-sipping business."

"I would be glad to discuss lachryphagy."

A flutter of hope stirred in Floella's chest. Mayhap, there was more to the pompous educator than she had suspected. Maybe, she wouldn't have to make an immutable choice today.

"There doesn't seem to be any mystery here," said Professor Bogdan between sips of Earl Grey. "Tear-sippers do it for salt. I have read articles about Brazilian *Gorgone macarea* moths drinking tears from sleeping birds. It is old news. Nothing worthy of a research grant. And certainly not worth the funds necessary to send you traipsing about Brazil studying moths."

"I disagree," said Floella in her most pleasant voice. "Granted the salts in tears give the moths a nutrient necessary for successful reproduction. Salts, I might add, which are not available in nectar. But I believe tear-sipping moths are also looking for albumin and..."

"Nonsense," huffed Wallace Bogdan.

Trying to control her temper, Floella dug her fingernails into her palm. She felt a muscle tighten and release repeatedly beneath her left eye.

"It is all about salt," stated Bogdan as a chunk of shortbread fell from the corner of his mouth and joined the crumbs littering his vest. "Needing salt, Asian *Lobocraspis griseifusa* moths locate an acceptable roosting bird. Next, they perch on the bird's neck, insert their proboscis between the avian's eyelids and into its eyes, then suck out tears. I find the behavior far from fascinating. It is revolting!"

"Actually, tear-sipping is quite practical," argued Floella. "I might remind you that moths also need globulin for longevity. Globulin is readily available in bird tears."

Professor Bogdan dismissed her words with a "Tut tut," and a wave of his hand. "I suppose Asia is also on your list of places to visit whilst researching tear-feeding moths?"

"It would be ideal to visit the moths which practice this behavior in their native environments. *Gorgone macarea* and *Lobocraspis griseifusa* are only two of the species involved."

"Revolting!" repeated Bogdan before licking the remaining cookie bits from his fingers.

"But you haven't even looked at my notes," Floella protested. She patted a binder on her desk. "I'm sure if you take the time to study my completed research and my proposals, you will see the value in my studies."

"I don't need or want to." Bogdan popped the last piece of shortbread into his mouth, took a sip of tea, and resumed speaking. "Then, there are *Hemiceratoides hieroglyphica* — tear-feeders with barbed proboscises to hook into a bird's eye. So, you will have to fly to Madagascar and spend weeks, maybe months researching there. How much do you think that will cost the university?"

He might be a jerk, but he has certainly done his research, thought Floella. *Research to shut down your research*, she reminded herself.

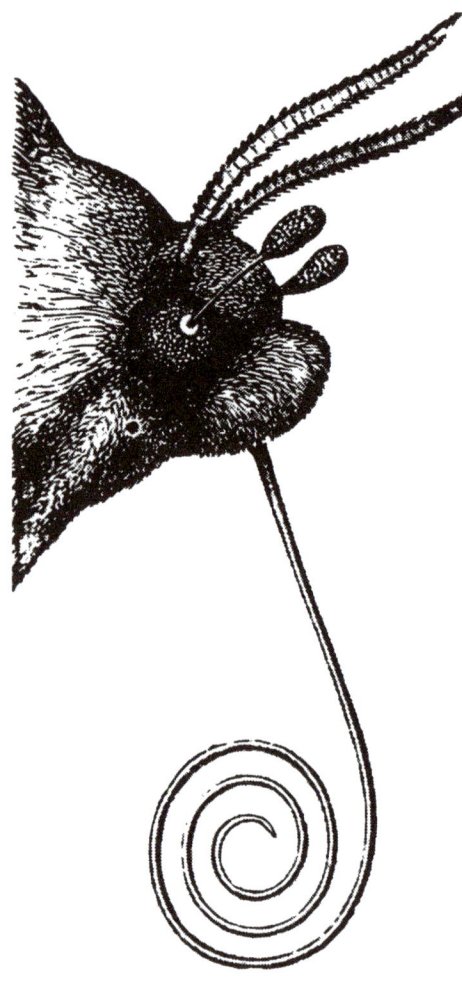

"When you are resourceful, it's amazing what knowledge you can acquire."

"I know it sounds vile, but the barbs are an evolutionary development allowing the moths to acquire the needed proteins with minimum effort. As an added bonus, the barbs also prevent the disruption of the birds' sleep."

Bogdan crossed his arms over his stomach and yawned.

Floella could see every filling in his teeth.

"Of course, there is the tear-sipping behavior observed in a variety of *Lepidoptera* species, both moths and butterflies, involving larger mammals like water buffalo, cattle, horses, deer, tapirs, pigs, elephants — even humans." Floella realized her voice had taken on a begging tone. She hated herself for it, but she hoped to avoid the next steps.

"Moths or butterflies, they are looking for salt," stated Wallace Bogdan with the confidence of someone who believes they are always correct.

"And reptiles," continued Floella. Still, she clung to a sliver of hope. "Caiman in Central America, crocodiles in Africa..."

"Enough, Flo," said Bogdan as he reached for another shortbread cookie. "I am *not* supporting your ridiculous research project. I don't think..." The professor paused, frowned, then said again, "I don't think..."

"Enjoying your Earl Grey?" inquired Floella Greer as her colleague put the shortbread down and relaxed in his chair.

"I don't feel well," he said. "I am suddenly weak and a bit dizzy. Perhaps you should call for medical assistance."

"You should be dizzy." Floella nodded her head. She removed a vial from one of her blazer's pockets and held it up so the light from the window shone through the amber fluid which it contained.

"It is venom," she explained. "You see, moths were not the only thing I collected this summer on my annual sojourn into the tropical wilds."

Head tilted to one side, mouth slack, and arms resting on the chair's armrests, Wallace Bogdan appeared unable to move anything but his eyes.

"When you are resourceful, it's amazing what knowledge you can acquire." Floella stood, then walked to the front of her desk.

Her colleague's eyes were wide open, and his gaze jumped from her to the door to his teacup. He was blinking rapidly. With much effort, he finally slurred out, "Why?"

"If you had been willing to support me, I would have dribbled the antidote into your tea. You would have been none the wiser, and I'd have found a different donor," explained Floella as she walked to the rear of the room. "Your cooperation would have guaranteed adequate funding for my field research, and I could have remained at the University."

"Donor?" asked the professor with much effort.

"Yes. In order to continue my studies, I need tears, funding, and your cooperation." She opened a cupboard door and sighed. "The New England winters are too cold for my moths to go outside to find tears from birds, reptiles, or mammals."

Unable to speak, Professor Bogdan blinked his eyes in response.

"As you can see, I have a shelf of terrariums filled with tear-sipping moths. I had thought to find an apartment in a complex adjoining a homeless shelter. I've observed many street people have weepy eyes and sleep deeply at night. Using air vents, it would be easy to send my moths fluttering off each night to seek tears. But with so many people in a shelter, discovery is always an issue. What if someone awakens? What if the moths cannot find their way through the vent back to me in the ensuing ruckus?"

Again, Wallace Bogdan blinked his eyes.

"So, I came up with another solution: attract a donor to my office, let my moths have their fill of albumin, globulin, and yes, salt. Then, when his or her usefulness has run its course, eliminate the donor using obscure natural poisons and venoms. To a medical examiner, it will appear the donor has died of a heart attack or stroke. Depending on which toxins I use."

Floella smiled. "It might surprise you to know what other uses I have made of my *Lepidoptera* holiday travels in the tropical and subtropical regions of the world. I've discovered that if you show interest and are respectful, indigenous shaman and herbalists will share all sorts of fascinating information on local hallucinogens, poisons, and natural remedies. In fact, I completed a manuscript on the subject and sent it to a publisher this summer."

With much effort, Professor Brogan widened his eyes.

"As you know, publication is necessary if one is to rise in stature among one's peers at this university." Floella studied Wallace Brogan for a few seconds before continuing. "Or, at another more suitable institute of higher learning far from the laws of this country or time."

Without further comment, she opened the terrarium lids and released the moths. The whisper of *Lepidoptera* fluttered across the office and landed on Bogdan.

"I've been told there is little pain, though some eyeball irritation is necessary to stimulate tears," she informed her colleague. Almost as an afterthought, she added, "By the way, I *do* appreciate being addressed as Professor Greer. It is only fitting, as my credentials in Entomology exceed yours."

As the cloud of moths circled Wallace Bogdan's head, he squeezed his eyelids tightly closed.

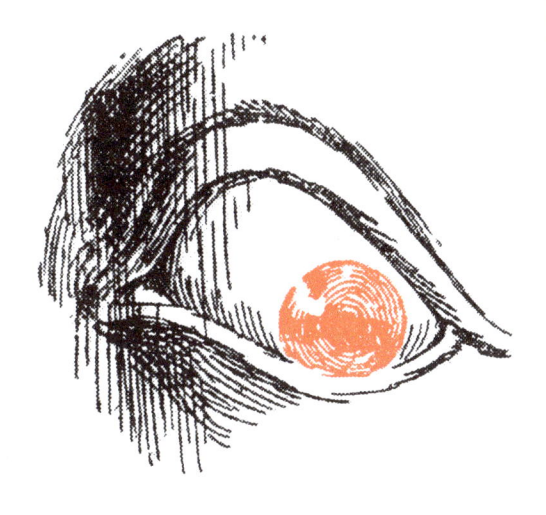

But as Floella Greer watched, the venom and moths won. When her moths were finished feeding, they flew back to their terrariums. Floella studied her colleague's face. He was terrified. She wondered if he was terrorized by the feeding, or afraid she would allow him to die.

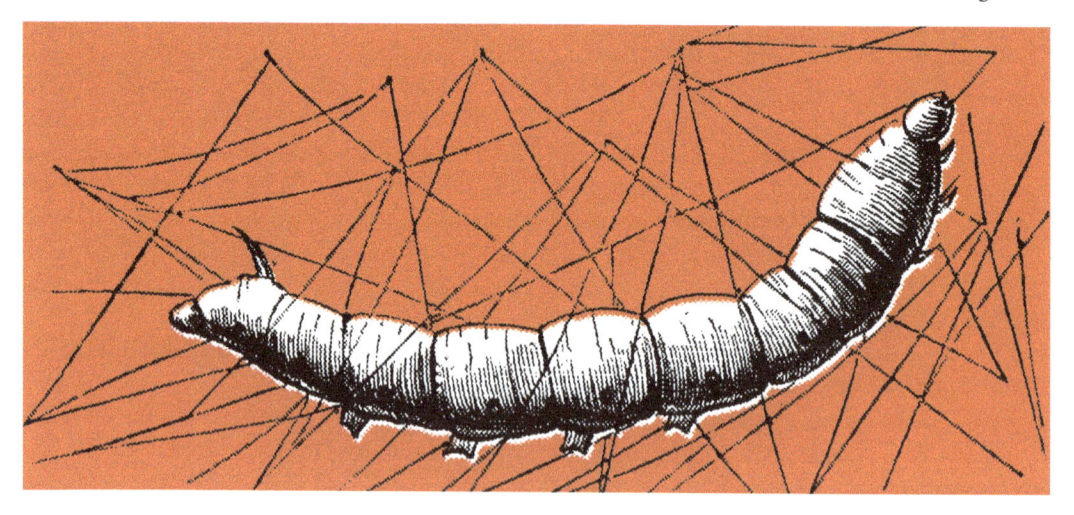

"Don't fret, Wallace," said Floella as she pulled a packed overnight bag from beneath her desk. Next, she picked up the binder containing her research summary from the desk and slipped it into her bag's side pocket. Then, she zipped it shut. Finally, she slipped the over-the-shoulder strap over her head. With hands still free, she went to her cupboard.

As the still drugged Professor Bogdan slumped in his chair, Floella loaded her moths into two portable, plastic containers. Though the tear-sippers were too tightly packed into the containers, she felt certain they would be fine for a few minutes.

"I will leave you to explain my absence," said Professor Floella Greer. She plucked a brown bottle from a bookshelf behind Wallace Bogdan. Using its eyedropper top, she squeezed three drops of liquid into her colleague's eyes. "The antidote will allow you to move in about fifteen minutes."

Wallace tried to mumble something.

"No need to thank me," she said. "You're just lucky I am *not* the murdering kind."

Then, humming happily, Floella grasped a moth-filled, plastic container in each hand. She walked out of her office. After stopping to close and lock the door, she glanced at her watch.

A ten-minute walk would bring her to the remnants of an abandoned stone cottage and garden near campus. Then, it was just a matter of stepping through a moss-covered arch near the rear of the property. She had discovered the portal while searching for *Lepidoptera*.

As she'd been observing a pair of *Celastrina neglecta* randomly flitting up and down, the pale blue butterflies had vanished when they'd passed through the archway. Floella had waited. A few seconds later, one of the Summer Azures had re-appeared.

Not believing what she'd witnessed, Floella had sat quietly in front of the structure and watched. About five minutes later, a trio of *Colias philodice* had bobbed before the mossy arch. Then, like the Azures before them, the Clouded Sulphurs had flown through the arch and disappeared. After four or five seconds, one of the yellow butterflies had re-materialized. Hovering for a split second, it had then descended to a nearby wildflower and alighted on its blossom.

Had Professor Bogdan been willing to fund her research and travel, Floella supposed she would have stayed on this side of the portal.

But it was now clear to her that in order to understand and protect her beloved tear-drinkers, she had to step through the archway.

As she stood before the portal, Floella saw grass, weeds, and forest beginnings which looked no different than those she observed on either side of the arch. She pressed her lips together, adjusted her grip on the containers of moths, and whispered, "Have faith. Have faith." Then, without a backwards glance, she strode through the portal.

Floella was surprised there was no electric jolt or cold breeze. It felt like she'd done nothing more than take a few steps forward. The grasses, flowers, and trees around her looked exactly like those on the other side of the arch. The only difference she spotted was a large flock of birds.

Frowning, Floella walked toward the forest. As she scanned the tree branches, she noted they were overloaded with hundreds of squawking avians of various species. Each winter, Floella fed the cardinals, chickadees, sparrows, and other cold hardy birds which remained in New England when robins and their ilk migrated south. *Her* winter birds were seed eaters.

But all the bird species she could identify among the screeching, feathered throng were insect eaters. An uneasiness washed over her. To release her tear-sippers here would result in their quick consumption.

"We must return home," whispered Floella to her treasured *Lepidoptera*, still safely held in their plastic cases.

As if they had understood her words, in a thunderous flap of wings the birds descended. Floella ran for the portal. But she tripped when a covey of quail dashed in front of her. When they struck the ground, first one container of moths, then the other broke open. Covering her ears to block out the noise of the feeding frenzy, Floella screamed as her tear-sippers were eaten.

Once the birds finished with the *Lepidoptera*, they turned their dark eyes toward Professor Floella Greer.

"No!" she yelled as she tried to get to the portal. The cloud of avians, which had grown to thousands of birds, blocked her way. Once the pecking and clawing began, she wept. With her moths dead, Floella supposed the birds would enjoy the globulin, minerals, and salt of *her* tears.

When her body eventually failed, Floella Greer felt her soul lift like a beautifully patterned moth toward the sun. But she was not alone. Floella found herself surrounded by an endless flight of *Lepidoptera* heading to warmer climes.

40

THE GHASTLING, BOOK TWENTY

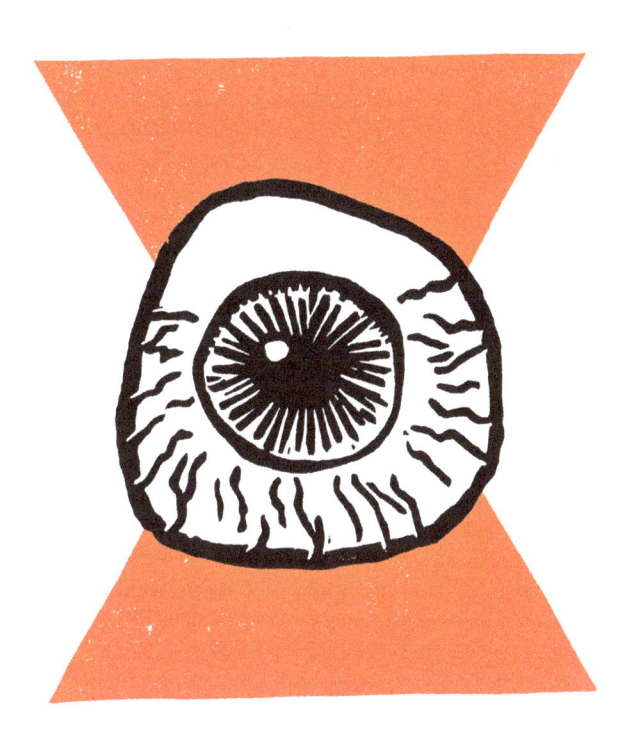

My Grandmother's Glass Eye

by Isobel Leach

The object she handed me was pearl-smooth and it slipped into my palm like a secret.

MY GRANDMOTHER'S GLASS EYE

It wasn't round, like I had expected, but I knew what it was immediately. My grandmother closed my fingers around it and held my hand for a moment.

I felt the soft fluttering of her pulse against my own as she told me, "it's yours now."

She tucked a strand of hair behind my ear, her fingertips brushing my right eyelid. My grandmother sounded sad — and it *was* sad, because that was the last time I saw her, though I didn't know it yet.

Everyone coveted my grandmother's glass eye, but none more so than me. The iris was the slippery pond-green of algae and just slightly brighter than her other eye if you spent enough time looking. Once I asked her if she could see out of her glass eye as well as her real one, whispering in her ear at the dinner table when it was time to clear the plates away.

"Oh yes," she answered, settling me in the crook of her elbow and drawing me close.

"Though you can't tell anyone."

"Why?"

She pulled back and looked me in the eyes.

"It lets me see invisible things," she said seriously. "But we can't let people know that."

Something about her words delighted me. They confirmed what I had started to suspect — that there was something more, something hidden and lurking beneath the surface of the world. I felt a smile widen across my face. If I couldn't have the eye, I reasoned, at least I could have its secrets.

"She'll be buried with it, you know," my brother used to tell me in the car home from our visits. As children, he initiated conversation with me only when it allowed him to enjoy the benefits of being the older sibling. "The rest of her body will decompose and all that will be left is that eyeball, rolling around the empty coffin. Like a marble."

Often, she would make me and my brother guess which one was real, and which was glass. She told us she could switch them back and forth at will, and each time I would wriggle myself up close to inspect the surface of each eye, determined to prove to her I could tell the difference.

"Please don't blink, Grandma," I would tell her, an earnestness scratching in my voice, our faces so close I could count the lines in her skin.

I turned my grandmother's head beneath the light to track the movement of the pupils, looking for shifts in texture as if I might catch ripples on the surface of a pond.

"It's the right one," my brother would always interject, though his levels of enthusiasm decreased over the years. My grandmother would respond, "You're very sure of that, aren't you?" and wink at him before turning to me, widening her eyes and lifting my hands towards her eyelids. "Why don't you find out?"

I drove home from my grandmother's slowly that day, the glass eye rattling in my glove box. It was disembodied — literally, wrongly — and as I drove I too began to feel I was missing something essential from my anatomy: the left half of my ribcage, maybe, or my tongue. The car dipped into a pothole and the glove box clattered. I blinked away the image of my grandmother turning from me, an eye patch covering the right side of her face.

As I drove I remembered getting in trouble at school, once, for telling everyone I had tried on my grandmother's glass eye and saw the devil. No one believed me, but still I took care to describe the process in the hopes it would render my story more convincing — the way I had lifted my own eyeball clean from its socket like I was collecting frogspawn; the clink of the glass eye as it settled in its place. I thought my grandmother would laugh when I told her, but the corner of her mouth pinched slightly. She took me aside later.

"I'm sorry for lying," the words tumbled out of my mouth before she could say anything. "I didn't really take your glass eye. I promise." Fear of losing my grandmother's affection lodged in my throat.

She waved it away and shook her head. "Oh, I don't mind that. I know you didn't take anything, darling. It's just—" she paused, her right eye lagging a little behind her left as her gaze flickered over my shoulder. "I wanted to be sure."

"Sure of what?"

She touched my cheek. "Never mind."

Her voice shook. A rush of observations followed — the threadbare mottling of the skin on her hands, the uncertainty of her step, how carefully she hugged me to her. All of a sudden I was worried I had scared her and I apologised again, quieter this time. Later, I remember wishing I had asked her a question — like whether she really was afraid or whether it was just my imagination. And if she was, of what exactly.

This question had followed me all through my teenage years and into my twenties. All the while, my brother moved further away and I moved gradually closer, keeping my grandmother in my line of vision as securely as I could. It was a concern, yes, but perhaps also a pull of curiosity that beckoned me closer. I became certain that my grandmother, and the eye, were hiding something. I still don't know if she would have told me the truth, all of it, had I asked.

❦

We spent a lot of afternoons with her after school. We would head to the lake near her house with a picnic, both of us taking one of her hands to help guide her on the path, or we'd sit around her kitchen table and make a game of reading out the letters from the pile that had come through the letterbox. I understood that this was as much about childcare as it was about my grandmother not being on her own.

Sometimes she'd say something odd, like "Your grandfather loves watercolour, too," while holding up her magnifying glass to a painting one of us had brought home from school. Talking about my grandfather in the present tense was a largely ignored behaviour of my grandmother's, given his death had preceded both of our births

"Depression. It's like winning the lottery. You achieve all your dreams, and then you realise you have nothing, absolutely nothing, left to look forward to."

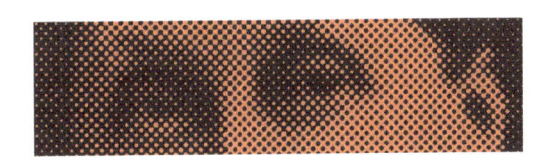

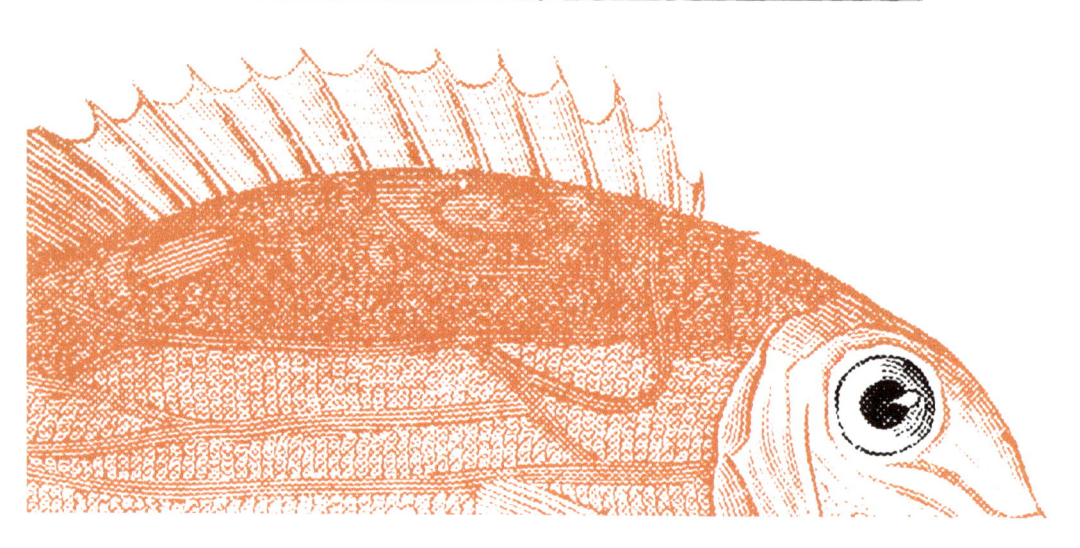

MY GRANDMOTHER'S GLASS EYE

by a long way. I was happier to look past this behaviour than my brother, who grew quiet and pale whenever my grandfather came up. Instead I grew louder, took up more space; the more of my grandmother's attention I could hold, the better.

When I got home, I called my brother to tell him about the glass eye and he laughed.

"I can't believe she's finally given it to you. You know what happens to people who get everything they've ever wanted, don't you?" His voice through the receiver was distant. Even from thousands of miles away, and with well over a decade to distance us from the reaches of childhood, he still enjoyed the authority our age difference let him claim.

"I don't, as it happens, but I'm sure you'll tell me."

"Depression. It's like winning the lottery. You achieve all your dreams, and then you realise you have nothing, absolutely nothing, left to look forward to."

I didn't know if my brother could recognise direct challenges any more than I knew how to make them, so I rolled my eyes, and ignored the pain that had started up beneath my right temple.

I put my grandmother's eye in my bedside table drawer while I decided what to do with it.

That evening, a headache set in — the world a half-hearted suggestion of itself in my vision.

It started as a tugging in the corner of my eye, as if someone had cast out a fly rod and the hook had settled itself snugly behind my right eye socket. I barely registered the feeling, odd as it was. But that night I dreamed vaguely of fishing lines. My mind started to conjure up images I couldn't explain: bloated, mangled fish caught on hooks, unblinking and thrashing beneath the surface, and fishing lines bobbing gently, serenely, in the water above. In my dreams, I longed for an eye made out of glass — something impenetrable and enduring, something the fish-hooks couldn't get.

When I awoke the next morning, I took the glass eye out of the drawer and held it in my flat palm, iris-up.

I thought of my brother's phone call the day before. I *had* always wanted the glass eye, that much was true. I'd spent years imagining what it might feel like between my fingers, whether my own body could be a house for it one day, whether it would feel cold and unyielding in my eye socket.

The idea of *more* control over my body fascinated me. The ways it could veer off course were deeply unsettling, and I had felt such satisfaction when trading the heavy periods and extreme pain of my teenage years for a daily pill that promised a cycle I could trust. The body was disobedient,

MY GRANDMOTHER'S GLASS EYE

I'd learnt; you could control it, for a price.

But now I had the eye, an unease tugged at me. It wasn't that I felt empty, like my brother had said; it was the opposite. I imagined the eye in my body, and it felt like swallowing something whole — something slippery, and hungry, and alive. Something that would grow inside me, bigger and bigger until it started to push out what was there already, until it got so big it would be far too late to stop it.

❀

The optician couldn't explain it — an eye pain was emerging — strain or weak muscles, perhaps. Without any double-vision or misalignment, there was nothing obviously wrong. But still the world got blurrier, and the people that sat next to me on buses took on an incomplete quality — most of the time, I couldn't quite be sure that it wasn't just my shadow sitting next to me, divorcing itself from my body and turning its shoulder to face the other way. I didn't want to look closer and check. Either way it felt like a loss: of my eyesight, of my capacity to recognise reality, of myself.

One evening, my flatmate suggested we turn our phones off at 7pm.

"No more fishing," she said gently, prising my phone out of my hand.

I had started to find it soothing to watch fishermen haul their catch onto their boats, to see the slippery bodies restrained in netting, slopping ineffectively onto the deck. I went to sleep with my hand pressed up against the socket of my right eye — a net, I imagined, keeping it in place. Just in case.

I didn't tell anyone else about the eye in my bedside drawer, or what my grandmother had said. I tried to convince myself it made sense for her to give it to me — that it was a gift, that it was what I wanted, and not a portent of what was to come. Later, I would describe it as a current taking me in a direction I hadn't anticipated, one I found I could not fight against.

By the time I heard the news about my grandmother, the world before me had folded over until it was a shortened, squat version of itself. The day of the funeral, I reached out my arm and could see my knuckles but not my fingertips. My brother tried to practise his speech with me so I hid in the toilets for an hour and scrolled on my phone — the clean, wet pop of a fish eye, the desperate thrash of the day's catch, the tell-tale signs of tail rot.

My grandmother's eye was in my pocket all day. I still didn't know what to do with it, and now a numb, crushing absence had spread in my chest. All I could feel was a tug, tug, tugging in the corner of my eye — the polite knock-knock of a guest, then someone pounding at a door to be let out.

❀

I didn't leave the house for two weeks. The headaches got worse. It had begun to seem like I was simply looking too much; all the shadows and tricks of the light hovering around me like traps; all the small pixels of the day pulling on my eye at the same time like they could stretch it out, pull it apart, see what was left. My boss called to ask if I could make it in for a meeting, but I said I was sick. I said the same the next day, and the next. I'm not sure how long I thought I could get away with it.

At this point, I had to trail my hands along the wall in order to get from my bedroom to the bathroom. Each time I looked, the hallway appeared to be a different length. Memories surfaced in odd flashes — the slow shake of my grandmother's shoulders when she was trying not to laugh, the coasters she laid out for tea, the light floral smell of the sheets in her spare bedroom. Other things I don't remember ever noticing: bannisters lining the walls of my grandmother's flat, how they scaffolded her movement from one room to the next. The mobility cane she wouldn't leave the house without. With each memory came a wave of missing, and I began to carry the glass eye around with me everywhere I went, convinced it would help.

On my phone, I brought up images of fish eyes, exposed and grim-wet and planet-like. I sent a couple of screenshots to my brother in the absence of any other social interaction. I started to think of my eye pain less as a misbehaving bodily reflex than a preparation, sleeping with the glass eye beneath my pillow. I began to wonder what it would offer me, if I asked.

My brother called me to ask how I was, which is something I could not recall had ever happened before.

"You're checking to see if I'm still alive, aren't you?" I was lying in my bedroom with the curtains drawn. I had called in sick to work for longer than I could remember and my flatmate had taken to tiptoeing around me in the kitchen and leaving me ice packs for my eye outside my bedroom door.

"Oh no, I'd never do that," he said, but I couldn't quite work out his tone. I wondered if he was thinking about the screenshots. "No, I just wanted to tell you I won the lottery."

"Oh really? How much?"

He paused. "£2.50."

"So you'll be OK, then?" I asked.

We didn't talk about what we learnt at the funeral.

I never knew much about my grandfather, beyond what my grandmother would tell us — how he preferred the lake to being out at sea, how he always came home smelling like algae, his coat dripping lakewater onto the carpet in the hallway.

My brother and I exchanged a glance when someone at the funeral talked not of my grandmother, as everyone else had, but of the man he had pulled out of a lake once. We found the speaker after in the corner by the door — an older man of about my grandmother's age, who didn't appear to know anyone else.

"You'll have to forgive me for speaking so crudely. I've never known quite what to say at funerals," the old man swallowed and the skin at his throat rippled in a way that distracted me, the flit of fish scales beneath the surface of a pond. "I knew her husband, see. We used to fish together and I was there when — well, I've never been able to forget it, that day at the lake. I always wanted to find her again, to apologise properly and pay my respects. And, uh, to find out what she meant, I suppose."

He must have taken in our expressions, my brother's face, pale and unsettled, I imagined a mirror to my own. He continued. The eye was cold and heavy in my pocket.

"She said she had a plan to see him again. She seemed so certain."

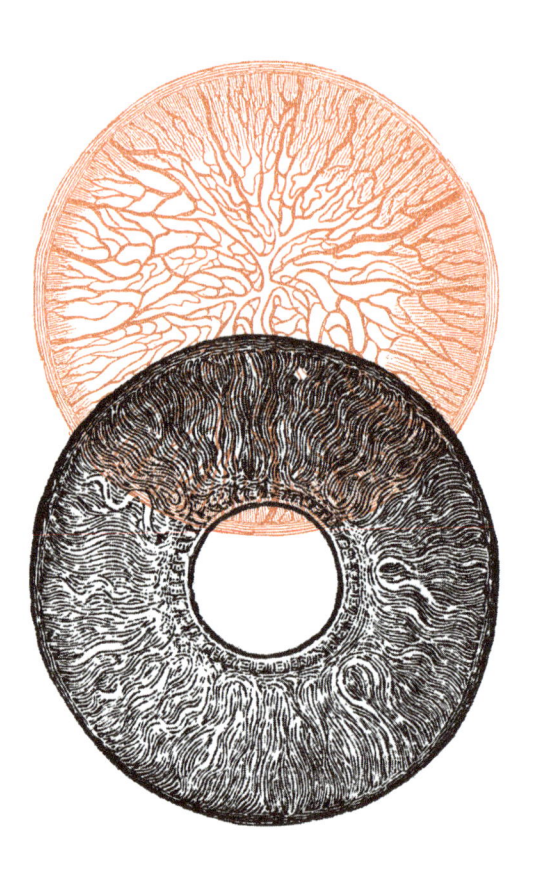

MY GRANDMOTHER'S GLASS EYE

beneath? This was my chance to seize back control of my body; all that was left was for me to choose.

I imagined it some more, but something had gone wrong somewhere, and I was still imagining it, wasn't I? The way my grandmother's outstretched arm curled into something clawed and shadow-like, the way its palm unfurled, the way it beckoned me forward, forward, chanting *payment, payment*.

The lakeside was cold when I arrived. The water was near-black and opaque in a way that soothed my eye. I took a step towards the bank, mud slipping up the sides of my boots. In my mind, I saw all the times I had watched my grandmother here, my brother and I squabbling over sandwiches as she looked out at something on the lake, a half-smile on her face. I pressed the glass eye deeper into the flesh of my palm. I felt my pulse tug against it, like something coming up for air.

The lake lapped at my feet, and I felt the water as if it was sipping at the corners of my body. I let it. I would gain so much, I thought, with the glass eye — my grandmother back, a hidden world. A dark presence crept up beside me, inside me, pushing up through my ribcage. So much, I thought, as I stepped closer still, to the lakebed, to the dark underworld of ghosts and devils it hid.

When I lifted my hands to my eye, I caught the last edges of the world in my vision and I remembered it for a long time — how the algae coating the lake had rippled out wide, and then the surface rearranged itself neatly afterward. The wake of a fisherman reeling in their catch maybe, or something else slipping quietly under. I imagined — my fingers reaching my eyelids, taking another step forward — that to an onlooker without a glass eye of their own, it would be quite difficult to tell.

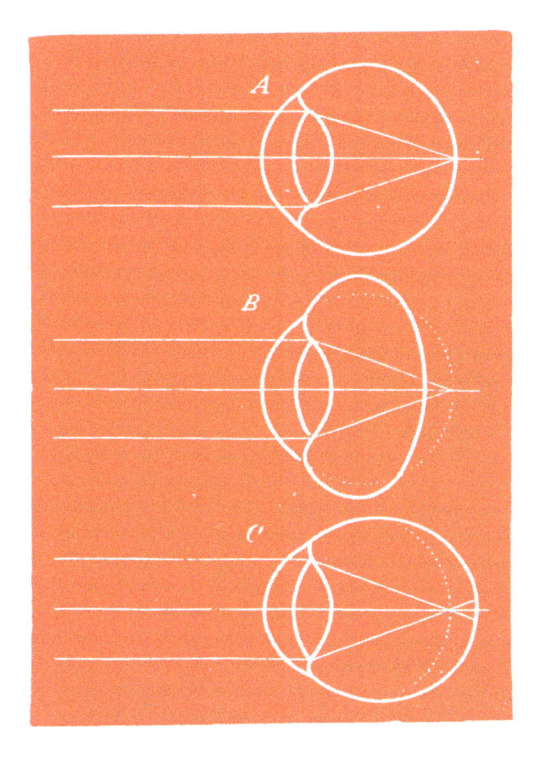

I moved my grandmother's glass eye to my window sill, propped up by a roll of sellotape, then to an eggcup on the bathroom shelf in front of the mirror. At this point, looking at anything directly was impossible — I engaged with the world a metre away from me as if peering through brackish water, looking for something long-buried in silt.

The bathroom light overhead trickled down my blurry reflection. I held up the glass eye to my own, green against grey. I stared at it for a long time.

So this was my choice, then.

In the space between one blink and the next, I imagined it — an end to the pain, a second chance at sight — a second sight, even, and the cool, smooth relief of the glass eye beneath my eyelid. I imagined it — the shape of my grandmother's arm, reaching out towards me. I imagined it — sliding a fingernail beneath the lip of the world in front of me, peeling back the surface to find out what was underneath.

I closed my eyes. What cold bargain had she struck, what murky depths had it let her reach? Would I give it up — the surface, for what was

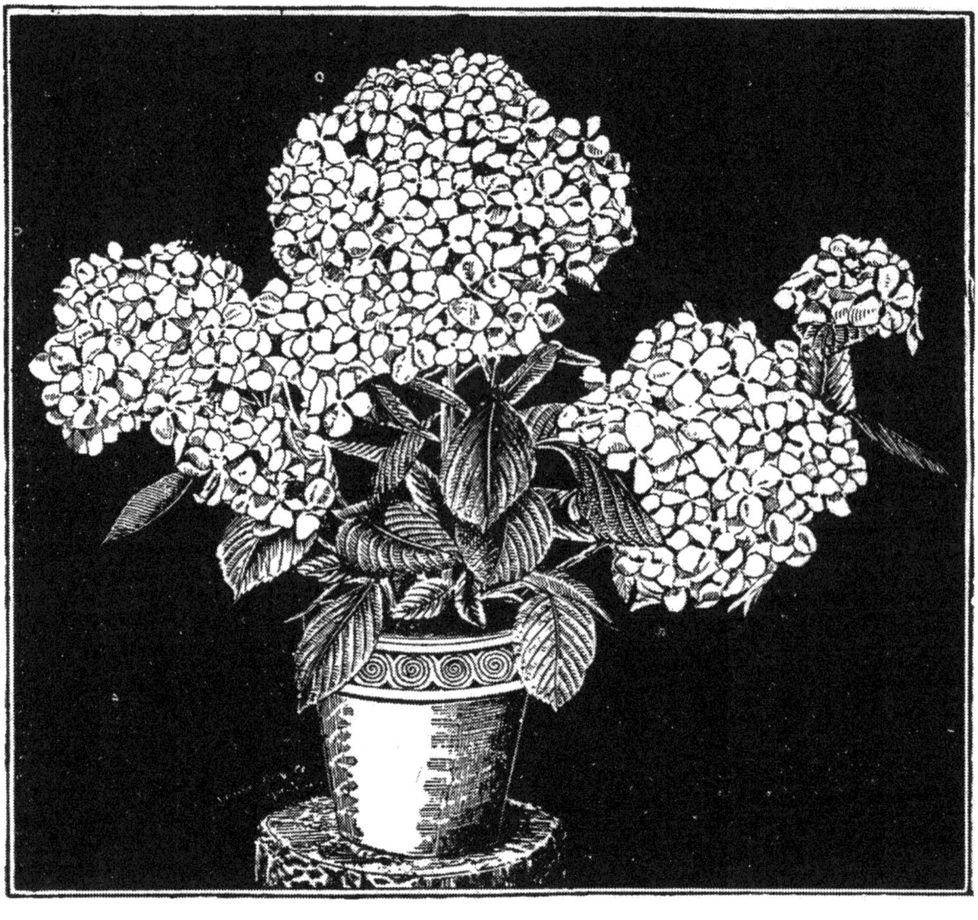

Freaks

by Fiona Cameron

*Laurel and I are freaks. Real freaks,
according to Spencer and his lot.*

FREAKS

Recently, I am beginning to think that they're right, but not for the reasons they think. Not because I have an uncool haircut and second-hand clothes; not because I'm skinny and awkward, and not because I'm just, well, me. It's because things seem to happen to us, to me and Laurel. Things that just don't make any sense.

They also say that I love Laurel, that I *lurve* her. They pull these stupid lovestruck cross-eyes at me or make lewd gestures behind our backs; tell me I follow her like a puppy and that it makes them want to puke. They want me to see, to hurt, to react, but I won't. What I feel for Laurel is something they could never understand. And I won't give them the satisfaction of the reaction they want; although inside, I am awash with a cold sort of nausea, and my face flushes crimson in shame every time they open their mouths or move to surround me in the common room. If Laurel notices, she doesn't show it. She'll walk right in, stick the kettle on and brew some of her funny herbal tea, all the while humming to herself. The girls of the upper sixth call her a weirdo, which makes no sense to me, because recently I've noticed some of them wearing their hair just like she does, casually swept up either side of her temples with combs, and some of them have taken to wearing red lipstick in a deep cherry shade, just like her. I think she knows, and I think perhaps she tests them sometimes. Like the one time she wore a thin red velvet ribbon, the bow tied tight around her slender neck — it was somehow magnificent, like regency style or, I don't know, she just looked so unusual, so out of time, the look became fresh. Three weeks later, Jaqueline Kenner appeared in the common room with a yellow ribbon around her neck. The other girls pored over it and congratulated her on her style. Soon, they all wore a variation of the neck ribbon, but Laurel never wore hers again.

Since Laurel appeared at school in January, she has made sitting these A-levels bearable. They said sixth form would be better; that things would calm down, that kids start to grow up a bit after sixteen, but they were so wrong, that is until Laurel arrived, and everything changed.

I ask her all the time about her old school, press her nervously about whether she will be able to catch up, to keep up? She just laughs and looks at me with amusement playing on her lips. If she finds me annoying, she doesn't say so.

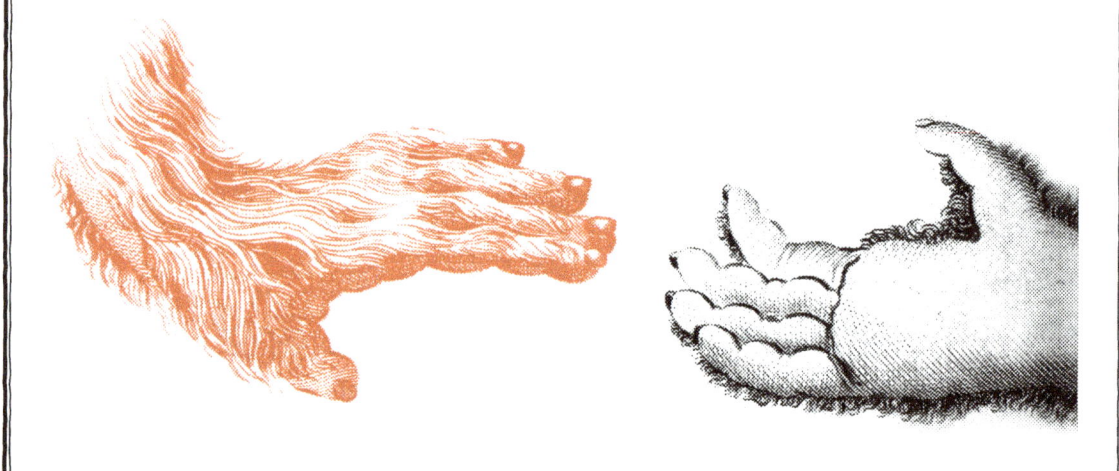

She and I often sit quietly reading under the row of lime trees at the edge of the sixth-form block. We walk home barefoot over the hard, tide-runnelled sand and let the cool sea air wash the school day away. At weekends I am invited to her large Victorian home where I meet her parents who are open and generous; they ask me questions about music and politics — automatically assume I'm going to university. Their book-filled living room is stuffed with plants and colourful rugs, there's a piano too. I am both delighted and bewildered by the attention but also deeply ashamed of how I mentally delete my mother's tiny flat from my mind and visually gorge myself on their world.

Laurel shrugs when I tell her she is lucky. She shrugs a lot. It's a habit she has. As is her finger clicking. She'll snap her fingers and laugh, come *on* Billy-o, she'll say. Billy-o Billy-o! You know the answer, Billy, we looked at this in class last week. Wakey wakey! She's teasing me, I know, but I like it. She's not being mean; it's just her way.

The first time the thing happens is one day in the spring term after she arrived. We are lying in the cool shade beneath the lime trees; it is becoming our habit. She, on her back, one leg crossed over the other. She is bouncing her foot as she reads, beating out a rhythm — her lips move silently as they toy with sentence after sentence. I'm aware I'm feeling happy, happy but sleepy, and I will myself to stay awake. Half because I want to watch her and half because I fear the approach of Spencer and his gang, they have the power to smash our idyll, or at least try to. I'm only just beginning to understand that Laurel isn't intimidated by them in the slightest and maybe it is this slow dawning; the realisation that I am safer with her now, that starts to help lull me, help me begin to drift off there and then on the dry stubbly grass. I gaze upwards, through the flickering patterns of leaves and hear a soft hum from her direction, and then something changes. It's almost imperceptible at first, perhaps something to do with the quivering quality of light, but it is enough to halt my daydreaming. I turn my eyes away from the canopy of leaves and look in her direction expectantly.

She is still sat there, but simultaneously she is not. I know I sound mad; I know. How to explain? It is as if she has become an outline of herself, a sort of shimmering outline. Then she is whole again. Foot tapping and humming. What is strange though is that her book has gone but her hands remain in a holding position, her fingers turning an invisible page. Then she is gone. Properly gone. I spring to my feet, dizzy in the sunlight, and scramble through the line of lime trees calling her name and tripping over my shoelaces and her discarded sandals. Spencer and friends have heard me. They move fast across the playing field, sensing wounded prey, they shove me against a tree.

'Lost your girlfriend, Freak?'

I close my eyes and focus on the sweet smell of linden blossom. Don't give them the satisfaction.

> *"Lost your girlfriend, Freak?" I close my eyes and focus on the sweet smell of linden blossom. Don't give them the satisfaction.*

FREAKS

'O Billy,' she says when she opens her front door. Her eyes are sleepy and smiley. 'You found my sandals!' And that is that. I press her, but all she says is, 'O Billy, it's too hot, don't be a bore. Come in, have some tea.'

I watch, dumbfounded as one of the cats winds its way around her ankles which seem real enough to me. So, I sigh, step inside and tell myself I was dreaming.

Her parent's house continues to fascinate me. I am in awe of the strange and beautiful light from the sea as it dances across the high white walls and the lofty corniced ceilings; the sand that eddies and piles in the front garden amongst the sea holly run wild and the sleeping cats, the soft song of the wind chimes by the back door and the seaweed drying on the washing line. I think these sounds and images will live inside of me forever. I dream of them.

When it happens again, I am less shocked I suppose. I don't know what it says about me but I seem to be able to simply accept that Laurel will, sometimes, just disappear. Reappear. Shimmer.

In a few days school is closing for the autumn half term. The classrooms are starting to get colder; the wheezing heating system huffs out steam and while the windows fuzz with condensation, I stare out into the gloom at the line of lime trees, their leaves now glowing yellow and starting to curl. I think ahead to the weekend because Laurel and I are going to the cinema. This feels like a big deal. It's her idea of course — an Italian film — of course, but I'm nervous all the same, just as if I've asked her on a date. That's because it *is* a date in my head and not just a casual film with a friend as she undoubtedly sees it. She gives me no sign that I am more to her than a friend, but I turn through the possibilities in my head in a relentless cycle.

'Hey freak! Miss is talking to you. Miss, he's lost it.'

Spencer's face is up in mine now. The teacher tells him to sit down and shut up and I am suddenly back in the room, back amongst the dampness of the darkening afternoon and the clatter of the classroom, and now trying to answer a question from the teacher that I didn't hear in the first place. Laurel sits at an adjacent desk and smiles at me, mouths O Billy...

'Don't look to her for answers,' barks the teacher. 'I'm asking you.'

FREAKS

In the summer months, the town cinema is all faded seaside charm — its once grand pink stucco exterior is flaking, and its three screens sit mostly empty. In the heat, the seafront smells of chips and fried onions and the still air is punctuated by the screeches of children splashing in the waves. Seagulls appear and disappear again and again like magic tricks. The cinema is where I choose to hide, inside in front of a screen in the safety of the dark.

Tonight is different. For once, I am not alone. Here is Laurel by my side, queuing with me in the sharp October night air. There are three films showing tonight: an old classic, *L'Avventura*, which we are going to see; *Independence Day*, and something called *Courage Under Fire*. *Independence Day* is a big deal, and we quickly find ourselves amid a crush for tickets. Some people are dressed up in Halloween costumes and soon the queues are heaving with devil horns and witches' hats, warm beer and cigarette smoke. Inevitably Spencer and friends are here, shouting their mouths off and throwing beer. I look at Laurel and try to smile. She's oblivious as always, oblivious to the sense of threat that is woven into my every waking moment, the threat that tugs and threatens the core of who I really am, who I could become. I despise how I feel and here she is staring upwards at the constellations that are appearing in the night sky above us.

'O Billy' she says, 'are you excited? I can't wait to see this.'

'Yes,' I say, 'yes,' as I listen to the slap of the waves rolling and curling in the dark.

In the end it turns out that it's just us and an older couple for *L'Avventura*. When I try to pay for our tickets, the girl on the till looks bewildered at first and I feel myself shrink with embarrassment. Laurel leans over me and reiterates the name of the film in a loud and perfect Italian accent. The people next to us look at her for a moment before the roar of the queue continues, the till girl rolls her eyes, issues our tickets and we are shoved forward towards the popcorn.

We make our way to the screen doors and slide into the dark, warm seats near the back. This soft warm place is where I usually hide, but here I am with Laurel and I feel exposed, silly even. What am I supposed to do now? Laurel rattles the popcorn, says, look Billy, it's about to start, and there at the end of the column of light in which the dust flies, the film flickers into action and we settle to watch the opening titles.

I am not sure I like or understand this film. Laurel is captivated but I'm increasingly unnerved by the disappearance of one of the female characters. I offer to fetch some more drinks. Laurel yawns and says 'yes,' she would like that. She stretches her feet out and says, 'see you in a min, Billy. Don't be long, you'll miss all the best bits.'

I pull back the heavy doors to our screen and step out into the empty corridor. It is silent and feels heavy. Every so often there is a deep boom from the other screens — whole other worlds playing out behind the closed doors. I picture Spencer and his mates whooping and throwing popcorn, I shudder and make my way down the corridor treading the thick carpet towards the foyer. The girl who served us earlier is there with a boy, they are kissing intensely and unaware of my approach. I cough and they spring apart; he swears under his breath and lopes off.

'What is it?' She asks as she drums her fingers on the countertop.

THE GHASTLING, BOOK TWENTY

I make my way slowly back through the booms of the carpeted corridor, where the hot dust and the smell of bubble-gum is cloying and wedge my body against the screen doors while I balance the drinks and push my way in. As my eyes adjust to the darkness, I am aware Laurel has gone, just a shimmer remains in her seat. I don't panic. I just berate myself internally for being boring company. Of course she's bloody disappeared in a film about a disappearance, what could be more 'Laurel' I think. I slowly drink both our drinks, watch the credits rise and nod at the old couple as they pick up their coats and leave. I wait until the coast is clear and then exit quickly before *Independence Day* empties out. Sod it, I think. Laurel can wait, I'm not chasing her down tonight, not this time.

It's half-term. I'm much more annoyed with Laurel than I had expected, and I don't call round to see her. I mope at home and hold out as long as I can. By Thursday I am less cross and able to admit to myself that the most recent disappearing act is only really annoying me because at some pathetic level I thought I was making progress on our *date*. I make my way across town to the sea front villas and knock at her door, composing my face into what I think is carefree nonchalance, which of course she will see through straight away. The door flies open and an exasperated looking man with two small children clinging to his legs answers and looks to me expectantly.

'Sorry, lad. No Laurel here. Think you've got the wrong house.'

'But...'

'But nothing. Now bugger off.'

The door slams shut, and I feel myself shrink inside as I look at the rusting children's scooter and the punctured balls that lie amongst the sand and sea holly in the little front garden.

In class the following week when Spencer sees her shimmering outline like the trace of a sparkler in the night air at the desk she once occupied, he leaps out of his chair and stumbles backwards.

'Freaks!' He bellows in my face.

I nod sadly.

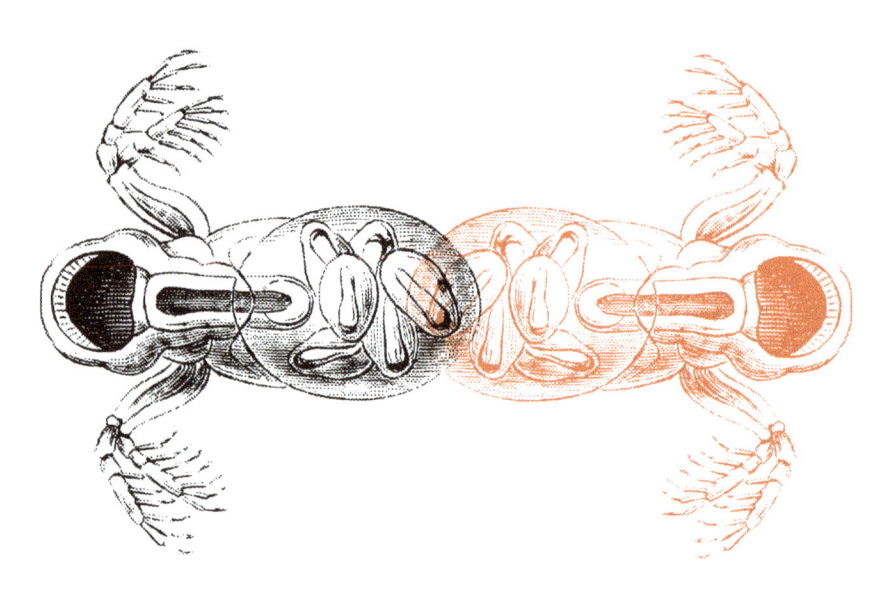

THE GHASTLING, BOOK TWENTY

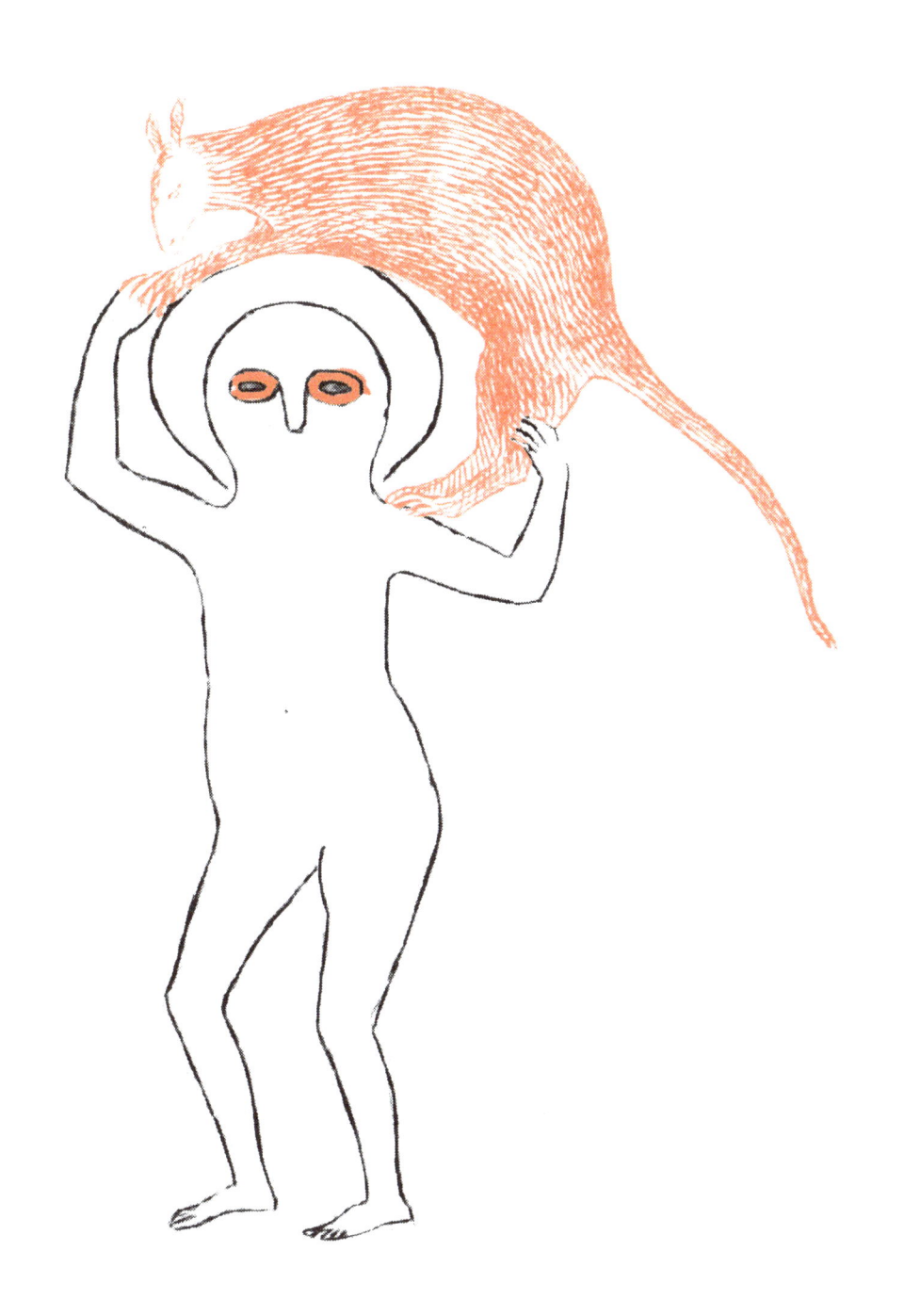

"THE SIREN AND THE BEAST"

Bramble

by Tom Preston

The bench was blighted by patches of cowering green growths, the wood uncannily smooth and fragrant with rot; a forgotten life, shrunk to the width of a dash between two dates on the memorial plaque, obscured by cloudy corrosion.

BRAMBLE

Sitting on the bench was Daniel, gaunt and indifferent to the wind, smirking from beneath the folds of his brown coat. Bramble was standing behind him, steaming Thermos cup clutched in both hands. The wind was sprightly today, and cruel. Below, the waves fawned over the rocks.

'You always arrive late,' Daniel sighed to Bramble. 'Have you changed those locks yet?'

'I've changed them a dozen times before,' Bramble replied, 'but the rust always comes back—'

'—and eats through everything,' Daniel finished.

'No question.'

'Have you ever noticed,' Daniel said, 'how the gulls never fly here?'

The kettle hissed from atop the stove. Miles, his elderly cat, ate his breakfast in the corner, paws tucked neatly beneath his chest. Bramble poured hot water into his dented Thermos and zipped up his Regatta jacket. An unmistakable chill was lurking in the corners of the house, barely noticeable for the moment — low beneath the skirting boards, clinging patiently to the ceiling cobwebs — but it had arrived, no question. Bramble went up to the chest of drawers on the landing. The air was changing already, he thought, a winking chill nudged inland by the sea, ready to repel the last of the noisy tourists and their oily sun cream; the city idiots who idealise the restorative benefits of living by the sea. What people failed to consider was the insidious stench in the air at low tide, of crusty fishing nets and decaying flotsam wreathed in shrivelled seaweed, and the insatiable rust that ate its way through every window fitting and door hinge. A more accurate description of living by the sea, Bramble thought, was that it was like salt rubbed into a wound that refused to congeal and seal itself shut. Always, it *oozed*.

Bramble picked out a maroon hat. Elasticity, long gone.

With the storms he had seen tearing along this coastline, he found it absurd that anyone could find peace here. It was pure violence.

On his way downstairs, he passed a mirror. He did not look. He rarely did, but in the fog-edged surface a small man with a mist of white hair around his ears passed through — existing, and then, very quickly, simply not — a face pale and slack, lined but lacking expression. Hunched. Frequently out of use.

As the land shifted in a descent towards the sea, curiosity paused Bramble and he looked closer at the prints pushed into the white sand. Small feet. The footprints faded at the beach, gone in a thousand possible directions. Grains of sand had swollen into pebbles and Bramble began to walk, feet slipping out from beneath him as he went, but that was unavoidable. No question. It made his knees chime with pain. Beverly Cove yawned out around him, Beverly Cliffs in the distance; beyond those tors sat another, smaller, cove: Dorothea's Pocket.

Dilbury crouched to his left, its buildings sun-bleached and flaky, subjugated by the wind. From the rotting boardwalk, a diaphanous figure in a yellow raincoat appeared to be watching him.

Beyond Dilbury, Bramble reached the cliff path, where branches of mountain ash curled around the muddy track like protective fingers. Twigs and leaves wove a net between the boughs so thick it felt like walking down a verdant burrow, patches of red berries splattering the walls. Emerging from the leafy tunnel, he came to the small outcrop that held a bench, on which sat a familiar figure in a dirty brown coat. Bramble took a seat. He unscrewed the Thermos and poured a cup of peppermint tea. The ground around the bench was covered in hedgehog succulents; a bumpy tapestry of kaleidoscopic greens and purples. The cliffs rose ahead of them like filthy teeth. The sea diced and thrashed below.

'He arrives late, as always!' Daniel exclaimed. 'You look tired.'

'Not the best night's sleep,' Bramble replied.

'Changing seasons can do that.' Daniel had a colourless face. He often — always, in fact — looked exhausted and malnourished. This aged him. His face was long and crooked, eyes deep-set, and he walked with a limp.

'I had a strange dream last night,' Daniel said.

'Hm?'

'I dreamt of the cliffs. *These* cliffs. They were *glowing*.'

'You what?'

'Something behind the cliffs was giving off this red light. It was strange. And a bit terrifying.'

'A lighthouse.'

'There's no lighthouse around for miles,' Daniel said, 'but how would you know that?'

Bramble said nothing.

'Boats don't come here, anyway,' Daniel said

'It must have been a vehicle,' Bramble said. 'Emergency services.'

'Those have *blue* lights.' Daniel added with a smirk, 'It was only a dream, remember?'

Bramble poured the rest of his tea away.

'I have to go,' he said.

'Already? All right then, Bramble,' Daniel said. He grinned. 'Why do they call you that, anyway?'

'I've forgotten.'

This was a lie.

'Hello, Bramble.'

A thin, flat whisper, drawing him from sleep.

Bramble opened his eyes. His room — cramped, damp and dishevelled, photoless — was saturated in an indifferent blue light. Dawn was about to crawl from the dark, the world still cradling a hazy memory of the night.

The fogginess of sleep dispersing, Bramble's eyes were drawn to the puddle of blackness between the bedroom door and the dresser. He stared, hard, into the darkness, wishing above all else the whisper had been in his dream.

Then, from behind the bedroom door, came a very real sound.

CRACK.

Bramble's heart thumped.

CRACK.

He slipped out of bed, cold snapping at his ankles, and approached the door. A turgid silence had filled the room.

Another CRACK, this time followed by a moist, squalling twist; something torn apart with inevitable violence. The sound brought Bramble momentarily to the butcher's counter when he was seven years old, just tall enough to look over the top at the white apron stained pink, cleaver thudding the wood block, hacking through the tissue and bone of inert hunks of flesh, long stringy white bits bouncing from the blade as it rose again for the next chop.

Bramble let out a shrill, defiant caw of terror and lunged for the doorknob.

The empty hallway glared back at him. Gradually, he became aware of a familiar hissing sound coming from below. Shivering, he went down to the kitchen. He removed the kettle from the stove, knowing he hadn't left it there. He knew that.

It *wasn't* me.

'Was it?' he asked Miles, who watched with lazy eyes from the counter.

> *Bramble let out a shrill, defiant caw of terror and lunged for the doorknob.*

When Bramble reached the beach, a cutting wind was dragging its nails over the cove. Pulling his hat low, he saw the figure in the yellow raincoat again, standing out on the sand this time. A quarter of a mile away at least, but the manner in which it stood, hood up and absolutely still and indifferent to the wind, filled Bramble with a dreadful chill that his hat and coat could do little to repel. The faceless figure was staring right at him.

Bramble hadn't realised how close he was to the water. He skipped awkwardly backwards to avoid the waves.

When he looked back up, the figure in the yellow raincoat was gone.

Daniel stretched out his thin arms and tilted his head from side to side. Bones in his neck and shoulders clicked. He reclined on the bench and grinned. His gums were bleeding as he said, 'Talking of tragedy.'

'What?' Bramble said, feeling a sudden and unpleasant lurch in his gut, as he realised he was standing by the bench. 'We were talking about that?'

'The pagans that used to live here,' Daniel continued, 'believed that when tragedy struck a community, it took on the form of an evil, vicious beast that would rampage through settlements and forests, scarring the landscape with blood and destruction. To repel the monster, a blood sacrifice had to be made to the siren, Dorothea, at the top of the steps overlooking Dorothea's Pocket. Once the sacrifice was made, she would rise from the waves, seduce the beast and trick it into drowning itself.'

'A blood sacrifice?' Bramble scoffed. 'Curing tragedy with more tragedy?'

'I suppose.'

'I was told a different version. The tragedy didn't create a monster. It created a mortal ghost, cursed to haunt the coastline, forever feeding on everyone's grief and misery.'

'A mortal ghost?'

'That's right,' Bramble said. 'A ghost that ages and withers, until it's just a skeleton wandering around scaring people. When its bones crumble and turn to dust, it gets blown around by the wind forever. The howling of the wind is the ghost's eternal cries of anguish.'

'Very poetic. Who told you that story?'

'Everyone knows it.'

'I like it. A rather apt metaphor for the destructive nature of grief. Don't you think?'

'I don't believe in any of that crap,' Bramble said. 'A fairytale. All superstition. No question.'

A moment of silence between them, buoyed by the wind.

'Bramble, are you alright?' Daniel said.

Bramble thought about the figure in the yellow raincoat. Then he thought about the noises outside his room.

'Yes, I'm fine.'

They listened to the sea for another moment.

'Tragedy can have a profound effect on the landscape,' Daniel said, 'whether you believe it or not.'

❋

When they were small, Bramble and his brother would sneak into old man Tavistock's garden to steal raspberries from the greenhouse. The garden was fenced off with tangles of barbed wire. Once, their mouths stuffed with juicy raspberries, satchels brimming with even more, Tavistock surprised them by thundering out of his cottage, swinging his polished cane for their heads. In their panic, Bramble and his brother dashed for the nearest stretch of wire. Bramble's brother skilfully slipped through the spiral of wire in one fluid movement but Bramble, who was too clumsy to master this particular skill, caught his sleeve on the way through, the barbed wire tearing through to puncture the skin. He wailed all the way home, half chewed raspberries still in his mouth.

At the time, he wasn't able to pronounce barbed wire, and the closest thing he knew of with similar properties was bramble, which from then on for the townspeople of Dilbury (with the help of his brother's teasing) became his long-lasting nickname.

❋

'Isn't it often the saying,' Daniel said, 'that people come to live by the sea to heal? To begin again after trauma? For some reason, they believe the damp and salty air has some kind of mystical cleansing quality. It can help them start anew.'

'I've heard that one before, yes,' Bramble said. 'It's nonsense.'

They were at the bench, again.

'I don't believe in any of that crap,' Daniel said.

'Don't tease me,' Bramble said.

'What people fail to consider,' Daniel continued, 'is the insidious stench in the air at low tide, of crusty fishing nets and decaying flotsam wreathed in shrivelled seaweed, and the insatiable rust that eats its way through every window fitting and door hinge. I think a more accurate description of living by the sea is that it's like salt being rubbed into a wound that refuses to congeal and seal itself shut. Always, it *oozes*.'

Bramble was standing. He raised a finger at Daniel and spluttered, 'Where did you get those words?'

'Yes, Bramble,' Daniel said, as if he hadn't heard him, 'rather like the slow chew of erosion of the coastline, living here is glacial, inevitable torture. Don't you agree?'

'I've *told you* about teasing me,' Bramble said.

'I have a right to be bitter about things, Bramble,' Daniel said. 'How long have you lived here?'

'I... I couldn't say for sure,' Bramble said. 'A long time.' Then he added, 'I don't like questions like that.'

Daniel laughed, his voice stolen, swallowed by the wind.

'How long have we been coming to this bench for our cheery little chats?' he said.

Bramble shook his head, eyes closed.

'What's your real name, Bramble?'

'Stop,' Bramble whispered.

'What? Hello? Bramble?'

'Stop it.'

'Don't tell me you've forgotten,' Daniel giggled.

'Shut up, will you?' Bramble said. Eyes still closed. 'You're starting to piss me off. Annoying. It's very *annoying*.'

'Hello? Bramble, *hello*?'

Bramble kept his eyes shut.

But Daniel was still talking.

'How could anyone find peace living by the sea? Look at it, Bramble. It's pure violence.'

Shards of spray were scattered from the ocean. Screams curling in the wind. The rain and the sea had bludgeoned the land into mud, and Bramble was sinking. It filled his boots and climbed up his chest, sliding over his tongue and compacting in his glowing red throat—

He woke, still choking before he realised he could breathe just fine. He relaxed. He exhaled.

He moved his leg, and felt the duvet catch.

'Off, Miles,' he grunted into the dark.

The weight remained.

Bramble lifted his head. It wasn't the small, curled form of Miles, as he had expected, but the silhouette of a person sitting there. Hooded and faceless in the dark. Bramble tried to cry out, as the dark intruder perched on the end of his bed raised an arm, yellow raincoat creaking with the movement. With a hideous, blunt crunch, the arm broke. A sliver of white bone shone through the torn yellow fabric.

'Who are you?' Bramble yelled. 'What do you want? Leave me, *please*!'

His hand searched beside him for the lamp switch, unable to pull his eyes away from the figure, from which now escaped a hissing whisper — *'Hello, Bramble!'* — as its hooded head tilted sharply to the right. The neck vertebrae inside snapped.

Bramble found the switch and spilled light into the room. The figure was gone. He reached out a hand to where it had been sitting. It was damp.

In the kitchen, he lifted a glass of water to his lips with quivering fingers. He leaned over the table, feeling cold and defeated, foolish — a silly little old man, thoughts grappling not only with the strange apparition in his room but the dream he had woken from just moments before. The storm over the cove — Dorothea's Pocket — the swamp of mud, and now he could remember the screams. All doused in red light.

Outside, the night was clear. He could see the abrasive lip of Beverly Cliffs in the distance. Then, a crimson glow rippled over the cliffs. Bramble backed away from the window. The light began to pulse over the cliffs again like a signal, a luminous red grin in the murk, beckoning him to the sea.

✼

At the place where he and Daniel would sit and talk, Bramble stopped.

The continuing path that disappeared over Beverly Cliffs, curving down to Dorothea's Pocket, was gone. A glutinous blockage of earth and stone had drowned it. Strangled trees and shrubs gasped for air and light in desperate, drooping green tufts. A disturbance had released a cascade of desecrated yellowish clay and rocks over the path. Aeons of sedimentary formation, undone in moments. The way to Dorothea's Pocket was blocked.

Bramble plunged his hands into the freshly exposed earth and began to dig; it was freezing, and it stank of compacted, crushing age. Dawn began to leak over the land as his crusty fingers found something that wasn't rock or soil, but synthetic and tough. It was Daniel's brown raincoat, and Bramble could see that it wasn't brown at all. The landslide had smeared away some of the dirt already on the coat. The raincoat was yellow.

Bramble's cracked voice bellowed out Daniel's name, praying that he hadn't been buried in the landslide, or swept into the sea. Strange and thorny though he was, and at times unpleasant with his words, Daniel was the only friend he had. No question. An acute shame twinged in his chest, but he couldn't remember why. When had he last seen Daniel? He called out his name again.

Then Bramble looked up, and two things happened.

At the summit of the landslide a thin figure appeared, looking down on him.

'Daniel! Is that you? Are you hurt–?'

The figure limped out of view, and the rain began.

And Bramble, quickly soaked and shivering, still clutching the yellow raincoat in his hands, began to climb. His muscles stewed and screamed as he crawled like an animal, more mud and rocks and uprooted trees coming loose, his every breath a flurry of cold needles to the lungs. But Bramble was beginning to see. He stopped to look beyond Beverly Cliffs, at the black clouds of the approaching storm, and back over Beverly Cove and Dilbury, which waited defenceless, as peacefully sublime as an oil painting. A land he had known for uncountable years, a life walking wooded paths and crooked gulches, wandering the endless beaches, leaving footprints in the sand no one saw.

Bramble lost his grip.

He dug in his fingers, fingernails splitting open, looking down at the constant sea and its slow, never-ending feast on the land. Daniel was right about living here. It did not heal or regenerate. It only consumed. Everything. Even memory. Bramble began to laugh. He was bawling into the rain as he climbed.

The storm clouds were closer, sucking the light from the new day. He looked up to the summit. A blue light was pulsing over the edge. Bramble dragged himself over the top and without the strength to stand, he crawled to the edge of Dorothea's Pocket.

BRAMBLE

The small cove cradled a weathered slipway, with stone harbour walls forking into the sea. The storm had arrived. Daniel climbed fluidly through the barbed wire fence at the bottom of the slope and stepped onto the slipway. The ambulance had skidded to a halt part way down, blue lights throbbing. Daniel limped past it towards the harbour wall. His exposed back was white and contorted, bulging in the wrong places, like some of the ribs were broken, spinal column crushed. Ahead of him, the storm curled into a fist.

Bramble began the descent to the slipway, legs burning with the effort of keeping himself upright. As he climbed through the fence, his footing gave way and he toppled. The barbed wire caught under his arm and tore through to the skin, carving a deep groove down his arm and through his palm, leaving ribbons of polyester and skin flapping in the wind.

Bramble collapsed on the slipway. Blood pumped from the long gash in his arm. He got to his feet and immediately reeled, falling into the side of the ambulance. A curtain of blood gushed over the blue lights, washing the cove in a crimson glow. Bramble managed a few more steps before he collapsed again.

In the mouth of the storm, upon the harbour wall, Daniel stopped and sank to his knees. As the violent swirl of rain and sea enveloped him, his form began to shrink. It was crumpling, atrophying, succumbing to the storm. Tissue, blood and bone, reduced to dust and dissolved in the wind; Bramble's despairing screams trying to follow with nowhere to go.

A slow, electronic beep; an inevitable rhythm, pealing up the walls of the cove.

The storm tears on in silence, as the beep slows.

Bramble turns from the harbour wall. The doors of the ambulance are open. They've loaded the gurney, wheels folded neatly underneath (just like Miles' paws), and he glimpses the broken form of a young boy still wearing his favourite yellow raincoat, before the doors are closed and the ambulance speeds up the slipway, bloody lights spinning in the dark like red lightning.

Every bone, they tell a numb Bramble, *from being repeatedly hurled into the rocks by the waves.* Tell him, a shivering shred of a boy, in a hospital corridor with his arm still bleeding through gauze, that terrible, incessant beep rattling his skull. Addressed by his real name, before he'd hide behind Bramble forever.

He always arrives late.

The storm, satisfied with its claim, had receded. Bramble was slumped on the harbour wall, haemorrhaging blood into the sea. His heart, already weak with years, was slowing, vision growing dark and thin, but he could see more now, see the strange inertia of his life; a symptom of unimpeachable guilt, an unimaginable grief masked and wrought into banal endless routine. Old man Bramble — real name lost, forgotten, or scratched from memory in shame — squeezed the yellow raincoat in his hands. He looked down at the thin skin and pronounced blueness of the veins. Slow rivers. Old man Bramble, salt in the open wound of coastline, a frayed edge of skin. He let the weight of his head curl him forwards, and in a quiet breath slipped into the water.

The beep lost its rhythm. Now, it was constant. A murmur in the wind.

THE GHASTLING, BOOK TWENTY

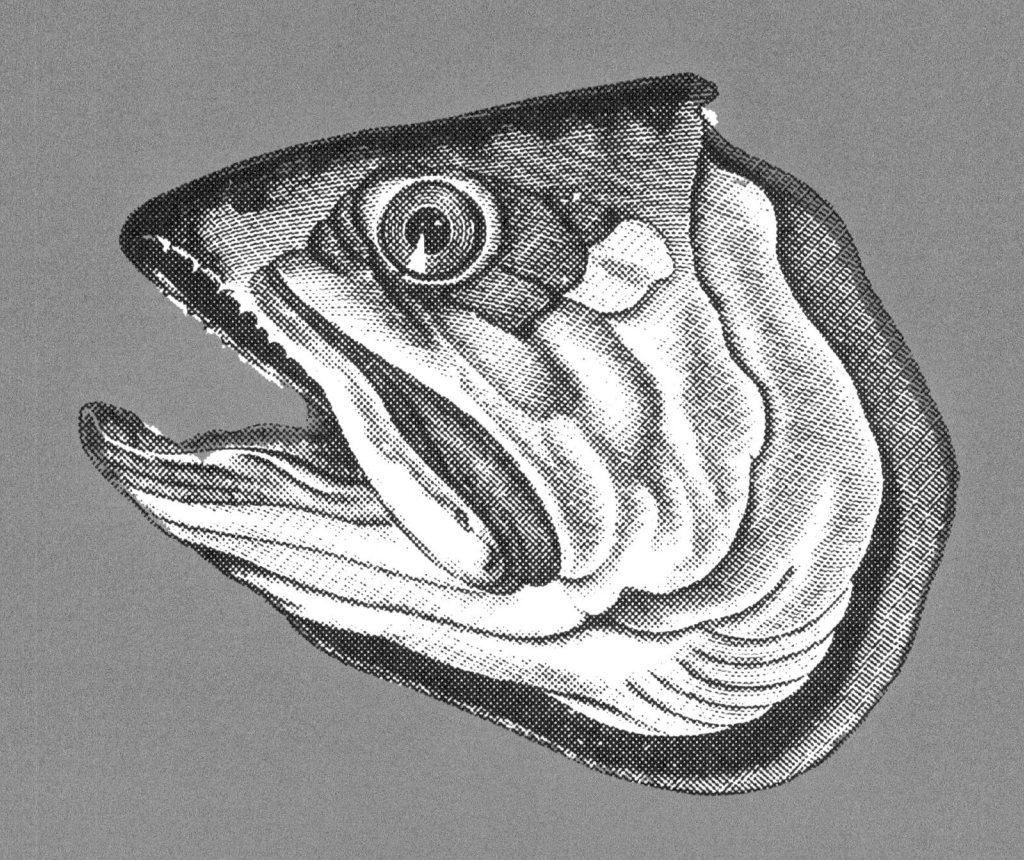

THE GHASTLING, BOOK TWENTY

Listening Wood
by Timothy Fox

The boy watched his father's hands pinch the limp rabbit's belly and tear.

LISTENING WOOD

THE carcass fell out of a pink mound of wiry flesh. His father held the skin; ran a wire through it, hung it up on the wall. He unhooked his knife from his belt and cut off the head, feet, and tail. He slit the gut and pulled out the innards. This he repeated with each carcass on the table.

And then he said to the boy, 'wrap them up'.

Before, the boy would have taken his time wrapping each carcass, carefully folding over and tucking them into the cloth, but his father grew impatient and said not to fuss so. Now, the boy reached for the cloth, covered the flesh, wrapped it once, and placed it into the basket. And then the two, the boy with the basket on his back and his father with his hands in his pockets, walked down the hill and into the village. They called on the inn, the tavern, and the wives at home. The boy waited outside while his father went into each place. And when all was sold, they walked back up the hill.

❋

His father struck his knife against a piece of flint, and a fire slowly awoke in the hearth. And then he lit his pipe and sat by the fire and did not move again. The boy climbed up to the loft and looked out the window toward Listening Wood.

All green and dark and silent. The trees standing tightly, one against the other, knitted together with vine and knotted roots. The boy had seen villagers come to the wood's edge, walk up and down seeking entry but finding none would turn back. Or in the gray of the morning, he would see burnt patches in the grass at the foot of the wood, as if someone had slept there in the night and then passed on. But he had never seen anyone or anything go into the wood. It remained impenetrable. Something ancient that had long ago turned its back on the world, hermetic and closed to man.

Where then did all the stories come from about the shadows and secrets and sighs that hid in the wood? The dogs that ate children? And how come the children called him witchboy? Had he come from the wood?

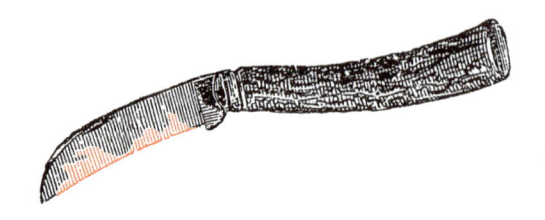

'Where is my mother?' He asked it simply, as if he had only become aware of the absence. But his father did not answer. 'Am I a witchboy?'

This made his father turn from the fire. 'Who says you are?' he asked.

'The others.'

His father bit the end of his pipe. 'What do you think that means?'

'I don't know. It's what they call me.'

'No, you're not a witchboy.' He turned back to the fire. 'Next time one of those shits calls you a witchboy, you hit 'em.'

❋

Outside, the boy walked around the house to the wall covered in skins. He rubbed his hand across the soft fur and willed them all to expand and fill and come thumping and twitching to life.

❋

He dreamed of the wood. *His feet were planted deep in the black soil. In a clearing he could see her crawl up naked from her den and stretch her moonlight white body. She floated into the air above the trees. He called to her, but she did not hear him.*

And then he woke to screaming.

He climbed down from the loft and crossed the room, careful not to wake his father asleep in his chair. He stepped out into the night. The screaming came from down the hill, and he walked slowly not to trip.

LISTENING WOOD

He knew it was a rabbit before he found it. Its hind leg caught in an iron jaw. It flopped from side to side, the leg pulled from its socket. The boy stared down at the rabbit, and the rabbit stared up at him. He wanted to call it by name, but he did not know what name that would be. He felt he must have known it once. He crouched down and ran his fingers through the grass, pressed them into the dewy earth. He found a stone.

※

He sat in the loft and cradled the dead rabbit. He hummed into its long brown ear. He kissed it. He put it in a box and slid it beneath his bed.

※

His father stood silhouetted in the open doorway, keeping out the misty morning. 'Did you go out last night?' he asked.

'No,' said the boy.

'I thought I heard you go out.'

'Maybe you dreamed it.'

'What do you know of my dreams?'

'I know I sometimes dream of things I think are real.'

His father took out his pipe and cleaned the bowl, eyeing the boy. 'Like what?'

'Things.'

'What things, boy?'

'About the wood.'

His father laughed. 'You only know what you've been told. Fairy stories. Not a true word to 'em.'

'I know about the wood,' said the boy.

'Oh, do you, now?'

'I know about the dogs that eat children.'

His father laughed again. 'That is true, that. There are dogs that eat children. And they'll eat you too if you're not careful.'

'Not if I take something for the wood.'

'What do you mean?'

'I've seen people from the village go down to the wood and burn things.'

'That's just their old ways.'

'What if I was to do that?'

'Well, you won't, do you hear me?' He took his seat by the fire and put his feet up on the grate. He continued to clean the bowl of his pipe. 'You won't be going down to the wood. Instead, you'll go down to the tavern and collect payment for me.'

'I don't want to go on my own.'

His father repeated his words, mocking. 'Go on now, boy.'

※

The boy did not enter the tavern. He stood outside the door, while the man in the apron stood within, counting out the coins. The man in the apron counted slowly, looking at the boy all the while. And having collected his father's fee, the boy turned from the tavern and found a row of children waiting for him.

'Witchboy,' they called out. 'Where's your mother, witchboy?' they shouted.

He was running as fast as he could, but they were close behind. And when he tripped and tried to push himself back up, the children kicked him back down. They kicked his legs and his side and when they kicked his belly, he shouted in great pain, his young voice cracking and screeching. The children stepped away, frightened by the sound, recognizing it for something that only children knew and adults had long forgotten. The boy opened his coat, and the dead rabbit fell out. It was stiff and smelled of death. He screamed again, and the children ran away.

'What happened?'
　'I fell on my way up the hill.'
　'Did those shits chase you?'
　The boy did not answer.
　'Did they beat you?'
　The boy was holding back his tears.
　'What did I tell you? Here. Come here. Hold up your hands. Hold them up.'
　But the boy would not hold up his hands. He felt limp.
　'Make a fist,' his father said. 'Make a fist, dammit!'

The boy made a fist.
　'Raise it up. Like this.'
　The boy raised his fist.
　'Now hit me.'
　'No.'
　'Hit me!'
　The boy hit his father.
　'Again!'
　The boy hit him again.
　'And again!'
　The boy smashed his fist harder and harder into his father's chest. His father laughed, 'Good, good!'
　Tired, the boy slumped to the ground. 'No more,' he said.
　'Where's the money?' his father asked.
　The boy reached into his coat, took out the coins and held them up.
　'What else do you have there?'
　'Nothing.'
　'What are you hiding, boy?'
　He put his hand into the boy's coat and pulled out the dead rabbit. 'What's this?' he shouted.
　The boy was silent. His father raised his fist.

LISTENING WOOD

She clawed at the dirt, digging him up, and he saw the moon and stars through the treetops. She whispered into his ear and held him. And from deep in the woods, they heard the howling of dogs.

He woke to the dead rabbit on his chest. His father was sitting by the fire, smoking his pipe.

'When a man goes down to the wood,' he said, 'it is because he wants something. And if he does not know what he wants, he does not know what he will get. And what the wood gives you, you take.'

The boy felt his head, the rising bump.

His father finished smoking his pipe and knocked the bowl against the grate. 'I went to the wood and the wood gave me your mother. I took her as my own. But at night she would go back to the wood. In the morning I would find her at the door, waiting to be invited back in. We carried on like this for some time, but soon the village took notice. Where had she come from? How long would she stay? Had I married her?

'I do not know who first called her witch. But the swelling of her belly in only a month's time was enough for 'em to start saying such things.

'She would have no midwife, she said. It would betray her.

'And the critter, all covered in fur that came screaming from her, would have done just that.

'She took it to the wood before the blood on her skirts was dry. I do not know what magic she performed, but the next morning she stood at the door with you, fair skinned, not like what she had birthed. And it were not long before they came in the night and took her. She cried pity for you, and they left you to me.'

'Where did they take her?' asked the boy.

'Not far. Down the hill. But she was gone soon enough. Each hand that held a bit of her was empty before they reached the village. The wood will not have taken away what it calls its own.'

'Why didn't the wood take me?'

'I left you at its edge many nights. I'd light a fire and ask it to take you, but always I could not stand to hear your screams or see you suffer. And I pondered how I would raise you, knowing full well that you would question where you came from, knowing there was some part of you that she had taken to the wood the night you were born.'

He picked up the flint from beside the fire and unhooked his knife from his belt. He held them out to the boy. 'Take these. No man can enter the wood uninvited. He must make an offering. That rabbit of yours will do.'

'Will I find my mother?'

'I can't answer that, boy. You may find yourself, though. Would that be enough for you?'

'I do not know.'

'You must know! No good will come from standing at the wood's edge and hoping for any old thing. You must know exactly what you want.'

The boy looked at his father and saw him as something incomplete. What had been taken from him or what had never been fixed to him was now lost for good. And the boy recognized this in himself. So he took the knife and the flint from his father and said, 'yes, it would be enough.'

As the sun set and a chill descended, the boy quickened his pace toward Listening Wood. He stopped where the grass gave way to the rocky black soil and the vines and the roots. He bent down and stabbed the earth with the knife. He kissed the rabbit and laid it in the little pit. He struck the knife against the flint, and the rabbit's fur set alight. He turned his eyes toward the tops of the trees, and the trees groaned from deep in their roots. The fire grew and illuminated the boy's face, and the wood saw his face and sighed. The trees parted, and the vines and the roots untangled. Black figures like dogs dashed out of the wood, and the boy shied at their sprinting touch, and the air was filled with howling. And the boy stood and stepped into the wood. And closing behind him, the wood sighed and snuffed out the fire.

THE GHASTLING, BOOK TWENTY

"THERE MUST BE AN OFFERING"

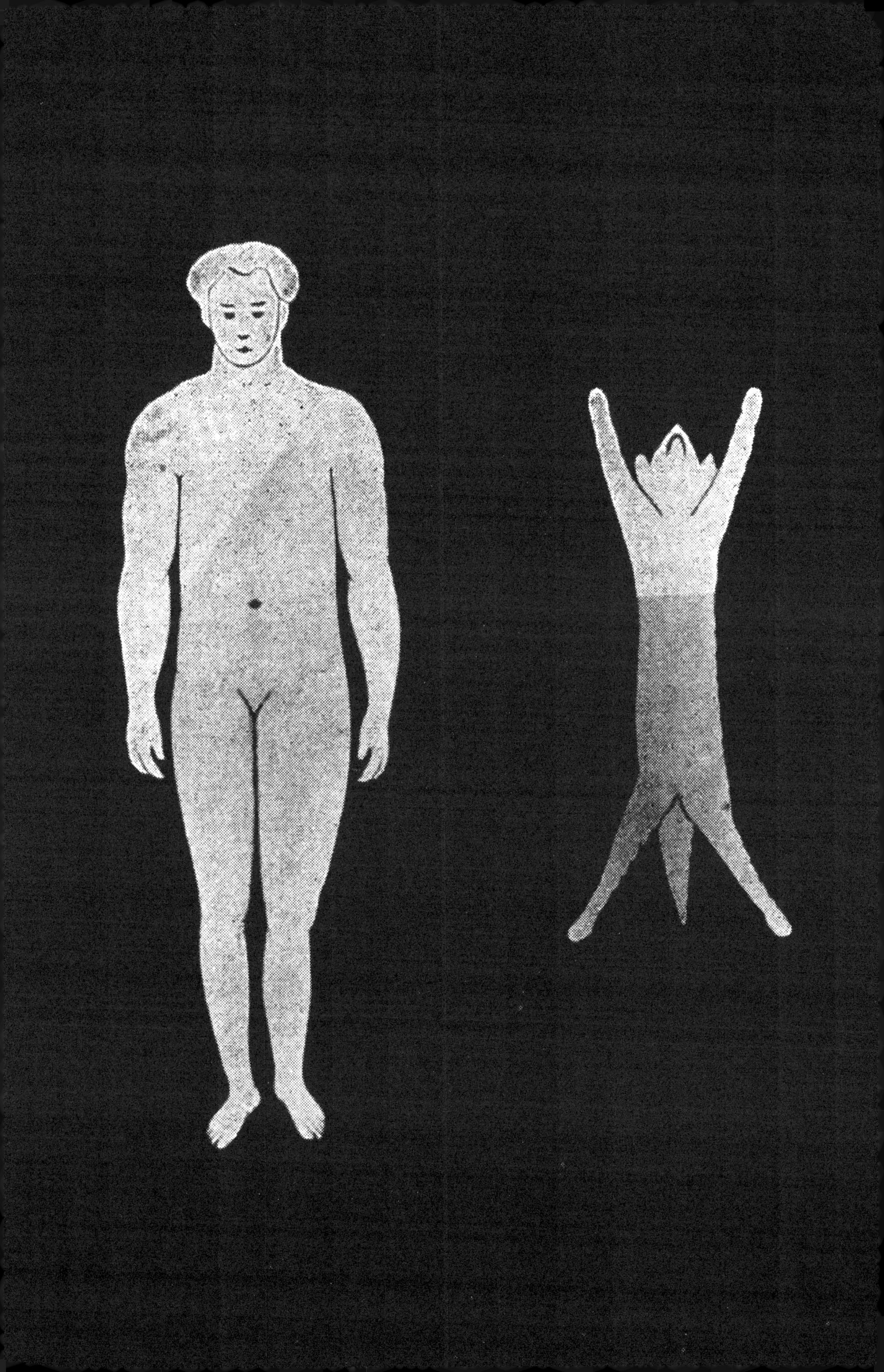

CONTRIBUTORS

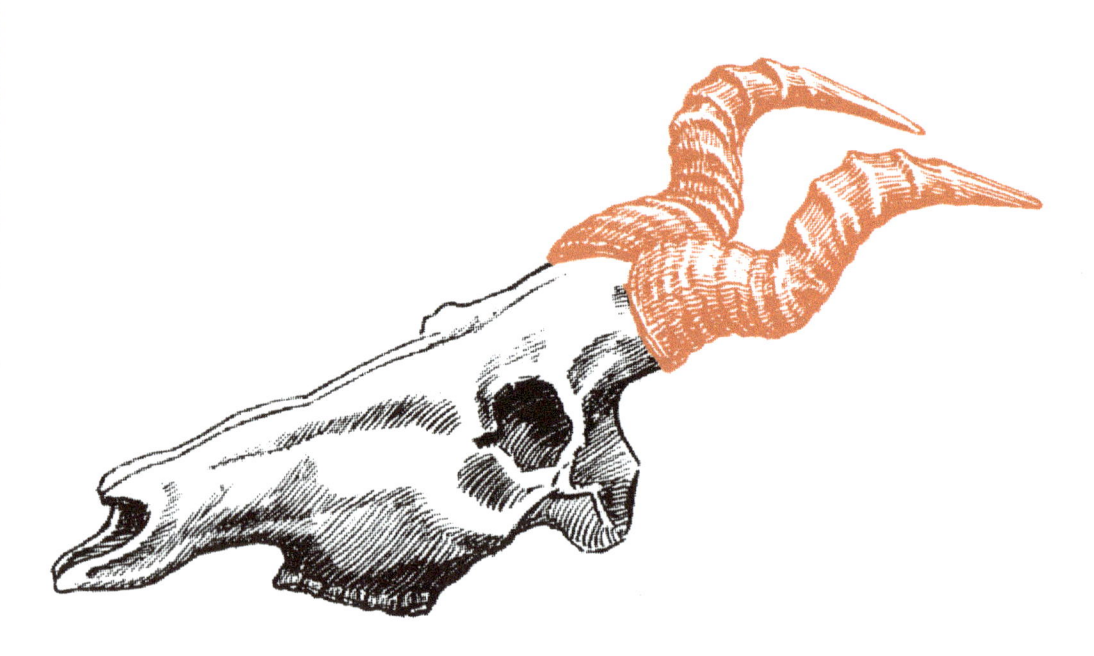

REBECCA PARFITT has worked in publishing for over a decade. By day, she is Commissioning Editor for Honno — the UK's longest running women's press; by night she haunts the desk at Ghastling Towers. She is a writer, editor and director. Her first short film, *Feeding Grief to Animals*, was commissioned and produced by the BBC and FfilmCymru Wales. She is currently working on a horror screenplay and a book of macabre short stories for which she won a Writers' Bursary from Literature Wales. Two stories from this collection were published in *The New Gothic Review* in 2020. *Rebeccaparfitt.com*

TRACEY REES is an aspiring writer of short stories and poetry. Tracey joined The Ghastling team as an editorial assistant in 2022. She lives with her husband and two feline friends near the whispering woods in South Wales, where she can often be found seeking out nocturnal animals for morbid conversations during her bouts of insomnia. When not busy doing those things Tracey is passionate about classic horror movies, spooky tales, travelling, drinking tea, and rearranging the furniture.

JEN SMITH-FURMAGE is The Ghastling's social media and marketing manager, a freelance publishing person, and feminist educator. Like most millennial horror fans, she started reading Stephen King at an inappropriately early age and now worships at the altar of Shirley Jackson, Catriona Ward and Mike Flanagan. Jen lives in South West England (she could probably throw you to Avebury Stone Circle from her house) with her black pug and brood of unruly children.

ANDREW ROBINSON is a printmaker and graphic designer. A self-taught artist specialising in linocut prints, his interests and influences stem from wildlife, printed ephemera, mythology, and all things creepy or otherworldly. Andrew inhabits the eastern woods of Canada with his partner and two daughters. *monografik.ca*.

CONTRIBUTORS

HEATHER PARR is a printmaker, working mainly in linocut, and her work often explores fortean and gothic themes. She lives in Brighton with her partner, daughter and cat and when she's not printing she works for a nature conservation charity.
Instagram: @xheatherlydiax
Etsy shop: etsy.com/uk/shop/nothingtralala

N.J. CARRÉ lives in Ireland, walking pathways that inspire strange stories of liminal places and people. When the forests, bogs and hedgerows allow, he works independently in the book trade.

J.P. RELPH is a Cumbrian writer hindered by a chronic health condition and four cats. Tea helps. She hunts in charity shops for haunted objects. JP writes about apocalypses a lot (despite not having the knees for one) and her collection of post-apoc short fiction, *Know That We Held* is available on Amazon. She recently got a zombie story onto the Wigleaf Top 50 longlist.

JOSH HANSON is the author of the novels *King's Hill*, *The Woodcutters*, as well as *Fortress* and *Caliope Street* (both forthcoming), as well as the novelette, *Marshbank*. He lives in northern Wyoming where he teaches, writes, and makes up little songs. His short fiction has appeared or is forthcoming in various anthologies as well as *The Deeps*, *The HorrorZine*, *Siren's Call*, *The Chamber*, *BlackPetals*, and others.

AVA DEVRIES writes about the weird, the uncanny, and the abject. She holds a BA in Creative Writing from Western Washington University, where she's also starting the MA program this fall. Ava is a Submissions Reader for *Fusion Fragment* and the Lead Fiction Editor at *Beneath the Garden*. Her fiction has appeared in *Crow & Cross Keys* and Broken Antler's *BAM Quarterly*. She can be found @ava_devries on Instagram and @AvaDeVries04 on Twitter.

VONNIE WINSLOW CRIST, SFWA, HWA, is author of *Shivers, Scares, and Goosebumps*, *Dragon Rain*, *Beneath Raven's Wing*, *The Enchanted Dagger*, *Owl Light*, *The Greener Forest*, and other award-winning books. Her speculative writing appears in *Asimov's Magazine*, *Amazing Stories*, *Cast of Wonders*, *Weirdbook: Witches*, *Chilling Ghost Short Stories*, and elsewhere. Believing the world is still filled with mystery, miracles, and magic, she strives to celebrate the power of myth in her writing.

ISOBEL LEACH lives in London and writes stories about ghosts — even though she's scared of the dark. This would be her first publication.

FIONA CAMERON is a poet and short story writer and teaches Creative Writing at Bangor University. She is the author of two poetry collections: *Bendigo* (Knives Forks and Spoons Press, 2015) and *She May Be Radon* (Knives Forks and Spoons Press, 2021). Recent creative work has appeared in *Poetry Wales*, *Strix*, *Horror Across Borders*, *The Lonely Crowd* and *The New Welsh Review*. Recently published critical work in the *Horrifying Children* anthology examines the female experience of the supernatural in children's/YA fiction and TV of the 70s and 80s. As part of the 80s generation ~~terrified~~ influenced by Usborne's *The World of the Unknown: Ghosts*, she still relishes steeping herself in all things strange as both reader and writer.

TOM PRESTON (he/him) is a writer from Dorset, UK. His short fiction has appeared or is forthcoming in *MetaStellar*, *Hearth & Coffin Literary Journal*, *Litro Online* and *Dagda Publishing*. Two of his poems were featured in Forward Poetry's 'Light Up the Dark' edition. He lives in London.

TIMOTHY FOX is a London Library Emerging Writer. He received a Vault Festival Spirit Award for his play, *The Witch's Mark*. His writing has appeared in, among others, *Denver Quarterly*, *Funicular Magazine* and *New Writing Scotland*.

G